THE CONTRACT

THE CONTRACT

A Novel by J. W. RHOADS

HENRY HOLT AND COMPANY
NEW YORK

For M. and L., D.L., R. and P.W.,
J.M. and S., F.S. and W.

Copyright © 1986 by J. W. Rhoads
All rights reserved, including the right to reproduce
this book or portions thereof in any form.
Published in the United States by
Henry Holt and Company, 521 Fifth Avenue,
New York, New York 10175.
Published simultaneously in Canada.
Originally published in Great Britain
under the title *Baudoin's Moustache*.

Library of Congress Cataloging-in-Publication Data
Rhoads, J. W.
The contract.
I. Title.
PR6068.H5B3   1986   823'.914   85-24908
ISBN: 0-03-008082-7

First American Edition

Printed in the United States of America
1 3 5 7 9 10 8 6 4 2

ISBN 0-03-008082-7

1

'If the *viagère** has been a favourite comic theme for literature, the theatre and film – because speculation on death, along with cuckoldry, has always inspired laughter – one must remember that it has also been condemned as a practice that encourages murder.'

La Vie Contemporaine

*viagère: literally for life, lifetime; that venerable French system of property transfer whereby the purchaser, dubbed the *débirentier* in French, guarantees the vendor (*vendeur*) – usually an elderly person without heirs – a lifetime annual annuity in exchange for eventual title to the *vendeur*'s property at his or her decease. The longer the *vendeur* lives the more costly the property – and of course, vice versa.

Baudoin picked up the document and waded once again through the ponderous sonorities of its legal French: '. . . The purchaser hereby covenants with the vendor to pay and discharge the aforementioned amount in the form of a life annuity paid out in annual instalments, the benefit of which shall accrue to the vendor during the remainder of her lifetime. The purchaser hereby undertakes and obliges himself to pay the sum of 3,500 francs in advance and a like sum thereafter on the 25th day of January, April, July and October of each year, to make the first payment on the 25th day of January, and to continue thus, quarter by quarter until the day of the decease of the widow Honorine Emilie Vallette, née Roussin, vendor, at which time the said rent shall be redeemed and amortised.'

His eye slid down to the dotted lines at the bottom of the page where his name and the old woman's had been typed in by Mireille, the notary's obliging secretary:

MONSIEUR RENÉ ROBERT BAUDOIN
BORN AT PARIS MAY 6 1917
. . . .
MADAME HONORINE ÉMILIE VALLETTE (NÉE ROUSSIN)
BORN AT CARCASSONNE JUNE 5 1887
. . . .

'Sign all four copies please.'

Baudoin took out his pen, and making a rapid series of mental calculations began to sign each document in turn: René Robert Baudoin . . . (1887 . . . bitter memories of the Commune and the early days of the Republic . . . thirteen years before the end of the century). René Robert Baudoin . . . (1900 to 1957 is fifty-seven). René Robert Baudoin . . . (fifty-seven plus thirteen is seventy). He glanced sideways at the elderly woman seated to his right who, having laid aside her grey suede gloves, was searching her handbag with those groping movements common to women of whatever age. René Baud . . . His ball point ceased to function in mid-surname and, accepting the notary's fountain pen, he traced the last four invisible letters in a lighter blue ink, giving his signature the effect of fading abruptly into the white of the paper. The notary retrieved his pen and compressing his slight paunch against his desk as he passed the documents, smiling again that oily smile he might have borrowed for the occasion from some provincial mayor at election time, offered it to the widow. She had found her own, however, and unscrewing its cap, began to sign her name in the space indicated by his hairy forefinger. Her bright blue eyes behind the rimless bifocals seemed somehow at odds with the almost unrelieved black of her costume . . . mourning donned early by most French women of her generation for menfolk missing in action on the Chemin des Dames or fallen on the Marne. She appeared more diminutive seated before the notary's heavy desk than she had in her *salon*, bending over the tea service, looking up over the glasses to enquire whether they wanted one lump or two. The flat black straw hat with its vestigial veil was relieved by one concession to feminine frivolity – a bunch of miniature red cherries.

The interview which had followed tea was for Baudoin – inhibited by nervous deference, a discomfiture he felt at poking into the corners of her personal world – merely a confirmation of the floor plan which he had studied at length in the agent's office. His impressions were somewhat hazy: a naval officer's widow living alone among her mementos – daughter long since married and emigrated to Canada; spacious rooms filled with heavy dark furniture and rather a lot of exotic bric-à-brac; silver-framed photographs on the mantel; high windows overlooking the boulevard. The view they afforded of the Boulevard St Germain was the mirror image of the one he saw from his own windows directly opposite across the street.

Madame Honorine Emilie Vallette, née Roussin, snapped the pen away in her black leather handbag and got to her feet. She offered her hand to the notary and to Baudoin in turn, declined a lift home, pleading errands in the neighbourhood, and was escorted to the door by the notary – who, closing the door behind her, crossed to a filing cabinet in the corner, changed his mind, and turning to Baudoin, was just about to say something.

2

The assistant director has just requested quiet on the set; the director has called 'Action!' and our next glimpse of Baudoin is a medium long shot. He has just put down his coffee cup to relight the longest cigarette butt of a collection in the ashtray. Details of his costume: length of cigarette, tousling of the hair, pajama collar up or down, have been carefully checked by the continuity girl to match a preceding or subsequent close-up showing a certain preoccupied intentness of expression. He wears a bulky black cardigan over his pajamas in lieu of a dressing-gown and stands in bedroom slippers before his sitting-room windows which front the Boulevard St Germain and overlook the building opposite. One floor below, just above the bare branches of the plane trees that line the boulevard, the old woman's windows reflect a patch of unseasonal blue sky, frustrating his attempts to peer through them into the interior. From the vantage point of his late Aunt Berthe, whose framed photograph gazed placidly into the room from the wall behind him, he would have brought to mind the skipper of some ill-fated tramp steamer − with an irremediable and mysteriously increasing list to starboard − nervously pacing the bridge and scanning the horizon for a plume of smoke (the double of the one which trailed from his cigarette) signalling the arrival of an overdue rescue vessel.

His vigils had been thus far unrewarding. Once he thought he saw a dim shape moving behind the gauze curtains and another time the vague outline of a figure looking down into the street – which must have been a temporarily displaced standard lamp or flower vase, because it remained stationary for a full five minutes before disappearing again. For three quarters of an hour one afternoon he watched fascinated as a disembodied hand wielding a white cloth polished window panes. It withdrew mysteriously from time to time into the darkness of the interior like an ectoplasmic hand manipulated by an unseen medium and then after a pause reappeared again at the upper part of the next, continuing the same circular motion as it wiped its way methodically downward. He was not even sure that the hand belonged to the widow. She would have had to balance precariously on a chair or a rickety step-ladder to reach that height: a dangerous practice for a fragile old woman . . . Somewhere in his papers was an article clipped from *France Soir* with statistics about fatal accidents sustained by the elderly in their own homes. Perhaps now with his deposit safely in the bank she could afford a *femme de ménage* to do the heavier housework.

His curiosity on this point was satisfied a few days later as he watched a stocky, round-faced young woman with short cropped black hair working industriously at the window boxes – uprooting dead plants which she placed on a spread newspaper and stirring something from a carton into the soil with a hand trowel. Later that same day he saw her pause on her way out of the building to exchange a few words with the concierge who was then, as now, installed in her chair just inside the wide arched doorway.

'*Femme de ménage* comes Thursdays, 9 a.m. to 3 p.m.' Baudoin looked up from the notebook in which he had just jotted down this remembered titbit and saw that his own concierge had just crossed the street for a chat with her opposite number. She stood on widely planted feet hugging her bosom against the morning's chill, from time to time disengaging one hand to smooth her chignon. In finer weather the two often met halfway at one of the benches under the trees near the bus stop, occupying it for hours in lengthy business discussion. Their business of course was to know everyone else's business within the confines of their joint domain: specifically the two apartment buildings; more generally, a less well-defined territory with unfocused edges that subtly interpenetrated and in some cases overlapped the territories of yet other concierges, comprising a segment of the boulevard roughly bounded by the rue des St Pères at one end, the Place St Germain at the other, including ancillary transverse side streets as far as the rue Jacob and the Carréfour des Croix Rouges. It was through this informal but all pervasive intelligence network that Baudoin had first learned of Madame Vallette's apartment being on the market for sale by *viagère* – despite the gamble, his accountant advised, a better *placement* of Aunt Berthe's bequest and a chance to make the too-long-deferred transition from rent-payer to property owner.

Baudoin's coffee had cooled. He was just turning towards the kitchen when suddenly, as if conjured up, the widow appeared in the doorway across the street. She paused to exchange pleasantries with the two concierges and, net shopping bag in hand, a tiny black figure holding herself quite straight on very thin legs amidst the morning throng, passed on down the pavement towards the Place St Germain. Before he quite realised what he intended Baudoin had kicked off his slippers, stuffed his feet hurriedly into his shoes, got his overcoat on over his pajamas as he raced down the stairs two and three at a time and emerged at street level just as the old woman passed the terrace of the Deux Magots. She stopped at the corner waiting for a gap in the traffic that debouched from the rue de Rennes, giving Baudoin time to deal with a flapping shoelace that was threatening to trip him up – and to reconsider his sudden astonishing impulse. He straightened up, staring after her, wondering what exactly he thought he was doing, turned to go back, turned again and strode briskly after her on his own side of the street, buttoning his overcoat high at the neck as he went. In his anxiety to keep her short figure in sight over the heads of the morning rush-hour crowd (by now he had crossed the square), he almost fell over a pavement artist just putting the finishing touches to a pastel portrait of the Sacré Coeur. Baudoin had crushed one of the coloured chalks underfoot and, pressing two apologetic francs into the man's hand, hurried on down the pavement leaving a trail of heel-shaped sky-blue splotches. He saw, or thought he saw, through a briefly opening gap in the crowd, her spare figure turning left into the rue de Seine, arrived at that corner puffing heavily and spotted her standing at a vegetable stand a hundred yards further on. A swarthy shop assistant was still patiently bagging three of those and a kilo of that as he strolled by on the opposite side of the street looking for an excuse to loiter on the narrow pavement. A doorway offered concealment and he stepped into it, pretending to scan the row of tenants' names above a series of mail slots.

'... Montcalm, Violet, MacDougall, Balmoral, Harrison, Sarcelles, Abt, St Mandes ...'

At the name Balmoral the absurdity of his position struck him; by 'St Mandes' the exhilaration which had accompanied him gave way to a leaden ennui. What had he hoped to accomplish by pursuing her thus in his pajamas? Deduce the state of her health from her dietary preferences — carrots and leeks but never brussels sprouts? Learn that she preferred Brie to Camembert? Was a vegetarian? Squandered her modest new-found prosperity on *foie gras* or continued to buy *pâté de campagne* from long-established habit? Did she still drink an adequate *vin de table* or had she developed a taste for Mouton Rothschild?

He thrust his hands deeper into his coat pockets and stepped abruptly into the street ... straight into the path of an Afghan hound towing behind it at the end of a leash an attractive brunette. The dog saw an opening on Baudoin's left as its pretty owner tried to pass on the right, forcing her to embrace him in frozen embarrassment as she tried to disengage the leash from one hand and transfer it to the other in order to unlock the disjointed fandango which they now performed on the narrow pavement. Amid confused apologies murmured now into her hair, now addressed to her knee caps, as he frantically tried to disentangle his legs, Baudoin caught a glimpse of his quarry behind the reflection in the pharmacy window: she was handing a small square of paper across the counter.

The pharmacist disappeared into the back and she took a seat to wait. Baudoin, out of breath, was now peering from behind the rows of pastries ranged in a bakery window opposite – a hastily selected refuge affording a view into the pharmacy. Pretending to vacillate between the *mille-feuille* and the *baba au rhum*, he tried to visualise some quack's illegible scrawl on that small slip of white paper – which now reappeared from the back of the shop in the pharmacist's immaculate hand. The pharmacist shrugged a professional shrug and smiled apologetically – whatever it was, was out of stock; madame would have to wait a few days.

Baudoin returned by a somewhat roundabout route – a route which coincidentally took him past the greyly noncommittal façade of the Faculté de Médecine. He was licking the last traces of the *baba au rhum* from between two sticky fingers as he racked his brains for a stratagem that would give him a look at that prescription: *'Bonjour'* – brisk, professional – 'I am Madame Vallette's physician, Madame Honorine Vallette. My receptionist has given her a prescription intended for another patient which I must retrieve immediately.' Absurd. No doctor would call attention to his incompetence in such a dramatic fashion, especially to an inferior in the profession . . . perhaps a discreet phone call . . . a bit of professional complicity. 'I would just like to verify . . . etcetera . . . my receptionist is on vacation . . . etcetera . . .' No good: he would have to identify himself, and the name would have to match the signature on the prescription. For the moment he had no way of knowing her doctor's name. Too unusual. Too risky. *'Bonjour'* – friendly but a bit rushed – 'Madame Vallette asked me to pick up the prescription that she left here yesterday' (the day before yesterday?). 'No, nothing serious, just a slight cold I think . . . her nephew. I pass here anyway on my way to work.' Looking at watch, 'Good God, nine-thirty already.' Five minutes later he could dash back and return it. 'Sorry, but you've given me the wrong prescription; I want the one for Gallette, G.A.L.L.E.T.T.E., Miriam Gallette.' 'No? That's very curious, maybe she meant the pharmacy on the rue des St Pères.'

All he really risked was an embarrassing refusal. On the other hand the pharmacist might mention the incident, describe him to the old woman. There was also a chance that the pharmacist had seen him hovering in the street or witnessed the spectacle with the Afghan which happened right outside his window.

'*Merde!*'

A passerby looked at him in amusement and he realised that he must have exclaimed aloud.

3

In a narrow street not far from the Palais Royal is a shop with an English or pseudo-English façade upon whose *vitrine*, spelled out in raised white lettering, is the name Pembertin et Pétin (établ. 1898). Eye-level, mouse-grey velvet curtains suspended from a highly polished brass rod veil the interior. Nothing except a faceless china bust wearing an elaborate Louis Quatorze *perruque* suggests what might be sold there.

The bell tinkled as Baudoin opened the door and again as he closed it behind him. A middle-aged receptionist, wrapping a square parcel in brown paper, peered at him over the top of her spectacles.

'Monsieur . . . ?'

'A wig . . . I want to enquire about renting a wig . . . or does one say hair piece?'

'But certainly, monsieur. If you would care to take a seat through there' – indicating a doorway curtained in the same mouse-grey velvet – 'I'll send a designer to you.'

Spindly gilt chairs stood about informally on the reception room's burgundy carpeting next to small tables that looked too fragile to support the heavy leather-bound albums strewn upon their surfaces. A good many costume designers' sketches and framed photographs of theatrical productions ornamented the walls; more busts displayed period wigs. Baudoin had begun to leaf through one of the albums when an elegant young man appeared in the curtained doorway leading to the back of the shop. He posed for an instant like an *ingénue* making a first act entrance and smiled engagingly. 'And now monsieur, how can I help you . . . a theatrical production is it . . . a costume ball? Perhaps you've seen something in the album . . .' Either he too was wearing a wig or had tinted his own collar-length bob a fashionable premature grey.

'A disguise really,' explained Baudoin laughing a trifle nervously. 'For a costume party. Something quite ordinary but good enough to fool my friends.'

'Certainly monsieur.' The young man smiled as if anticipating the fun. 'If you'll just follow me please.' He guided Baudoin silently down a hallway decorated with antique theatrical posters announcing forgotten productions of *Volpone* or the *Malade Imaginaire*. Baudoin stepped aside for a flamboyant blonde carrying a cylindrical hat box who called something over her shoulder as she came out of one of the curtained cubicles opening off both sides of the corridor. He took the seat indicated by his guide before a dressing table mercilessly illuminated by vertical rows of bulbs on either side of the mirror.

'First to colouring,' said the young man and began to comb Baudoin's hair straight back with rather a lot of wrist action. 'Monsieur is quite dark . . . I would suggest something longer and lighter in colour . . . one moment please.' Baudoin was left to ponder his own unflattering image in the mirror and listen to the snatches of conversation which could be overheard through the flimsy partitions. 'Yes, Robert, it's the character all right but it's no longer me.'

'Precisely,' murmured Baudoin to himself as the young man's reflection, carrying a light-brown curly wig in one hand, appeared in the mirror behind him. The young man displayed it as might a head waiter presenting a filet mignon and slipped it deftly over Baudoin's own hair, patting the curls at the back with delicate little finger movements; then stood back, hand on hip, comb poised in mid-air, to appraise the result. A middle-aged pederast, entirely too dissipated but reassuringly unlike himself, regarded Baudoin critically from the mirror. 'A bit too stylish I think,' said Baudoin. 'I want to impersonate a drunken waiter who becomes increasingly tipsy as the evening progresses.'

'*Délicieux*,' squealed the young man, momentarily abandoning his suave professional manner and entering into the spirit of the joke. He produced in rapid succession a series of wigs which were slipped on, combed, patted, contemplated, rejected, slipped off, replaced and squinted at. A greying full shock of middle-aged dun-coloured hair (which incidentally gave Baudoin an uncanny resemblance to his uncle Rémy) was finally settled on.

The young man took a blue tape measure from the dressing-table drawer, pushing to one side a chart displaying an array of moustaches of all sizes and configurations strangely resembling a page of exotic butterflies. Baudoin thought suddenly of Aunt Berthe's attic in the summer house at Tilly sur Marne and himself as a small boy rummaging through the big old wicker trunk containing warped and disembowelled tennis racquets, an odd number of rusty fencing foils, and small bundles of letters (which could not have interested him then) tied with blue ribbon. Dust motes danced in the slanting sun's rays which made upon the floor a skewed duplicate of a small window high up under the eaves, and spotlighted the toes of a tanned, bare foot as he pored over the pages of a natural history for children – oblivious to the stale air and sultry heat . . . and the cold finger tips that now occasionally brushed his ears as the elegant young man manipulated the blue tape measure (coincidentally the exact shade of the ribbon binding the love letters in that wicker trunk), measuring in precise fractions of the earth's circumference, established with such eighteenth-century insouciance by the General Assembly in 1799, the distance from hair line to nape, from ear to ear, over the top of the cranium, from temple to temple around the back, and finally 'for good measure' said the young man, glancing into the mirror to see whether Baudoin had appreciated his little pun, the circumference of that smaller globe within which a series of alternative Baudoins were now taking shape: Docteur Gamelin with a precise little pencil moustache; Professeur Cendrar, silvery spade beard and distracted but dignified air; Robert Turin, a dirty and dishevelled *clochard* with a scraggly walrus and a cigarette butt tucked behind one ear pushing all of his earthly estate in a wobbly-wheeled pram.

'If monsieur could bear to part with his own moustache and substitute another . . . ' said the young man, who had noticed Baudoin's attempts to visualise himself sans moustache by holding two fingers over his upper lip, ' . . . he would be completely unrecognisable . . . these decisions, of course, are not taken lightly.'

There was some technical discussion about methods of attaching moustaches without resort to the elaborate manipulations with spirit gum that Baudoin remembered from his acting days at university. Time and Madame Q., his concierge, made quick change in the street, without benefit of a mirror, imperative. Feigning indecision, Baudoin finally took with him a full-blown grey walrus and an old-fashioned Hitlerian toothbrush. The wig would be sent on after alterations. He wondered what Gabrielle would think if he shaved off his moustache.

4

Outside, a gust of March wind besets the terrace of the Deux Magots, riffling trouser legs and pages of *Le Monde* and the *Herald Tribune*, forcing patrons to grab for hats and hemlines. Inside, amid relative quiet, Baudoin sits near the window and makes notations in a small black notebook. A Ricard and a whiskey stand untouched before him on the table. He is observed by Madame Genet, the cashier, who stands behind the *caisse* in her stocking feet – having kicked off her too tight, too expensive, new black shoes. Craning his neck, Baudoin can compare his wristwatch with the gilt hands of the church tower clock behind him in the square, just visible from this angle behind the scaffolding which obscures its façade. Across the square the same familiar pavement artist, hat pulled over his eyes, sits sleeping with his back to the church railings.

A young woman pushes through the revolving door and pauses just inside. She raises her handbag to grope inside for her glasses and as she does so its ornate clasp just catches the hem of her skirt, tugging it upward briefly to reveal a glimpse of thigh (not unappreciated by old René Hauterive, the senior waiter). Her expression is wan and pinched: its vulnerability emphasised by the characteristic nakedness of acute myopia. She holds her glasses up to her eyes lorgnette-fashion and sweeps the room looking for Baudoin who has just shut his notebook and returned it to his breast pocket along with the silver pencil. Gabrielle's uncertainty (for it is Gabrielle), the nakedness of her expression and flash of thigh, provoke a special surge of tenderness in Baudoin, who half-rises, smiling, and signals her to join him. She does not return his smile (a perfunctory peck on the cheek), sits with her back to the window in the seat just vacated by Baudoin, wrinkles her nose at the Ricard and orders a *vin blanc cassis* instead – something that Baudoin has never seen her drink in the two years that they have known each other. Madame Genet punches the cash register and wonders whether the girl wears her glasses in bed. She pushes her own thick lenses up higher on her nose and reflects that she hasn't seen a close-up of her husband's expression in ten years. The girl sits with her back straight against the seat and stares into her glass or peers blindly into the room past the gentleman's shoulder – directly at Madame Genet, as it happens, who divides her attention between the movement of the girl's lips and the slotted coin rack from which she unerringly selects the correct change for the waiters, placing the coins automatically in their black plastic saucers. The gentleman's smile has faded. Baudoin already wishes he had chosen the terrace where intimate conversation is masked by traffic noise and flapping awnings. He has captured one of Gabrielle's hands in two of his and holds it carefully as if it were a wounded bird. She ignores him and continues to speak, never deviating from her rehearsed recriminations.

'I simply don't believe you. How can you explain your wigs and moustaches and silly overalls? Whom do you meet at all hours? Why can't you explain it if all's so innocent?' Madame Genet overhears this much during one of those random silences that suddenly descend on a crowded room. Baudoin glances from side to side and protests in a vehement whisper. His hands seek to gesture more widely but inhibited by so many witnesses express his frustration in curtailed sweeps and staccato finger stabs at the table top. Old Hautrive transfers his folded napkin from forearm to shoulder as he passes the *caisse* and rolls his eyes ceilingward. Gabrielle presses on, oblivious of eavesdroppers – possibly because she cannot see them. The room is peopled by anonymous blurs which start to swim now as the tears come. One runs down her cheek and with a tiny inaudible splash falls into her untouched *vin blanc cassis*.

'*Je t'en supplie, Gabrielle . . .* This is ridiculous.' Baudoin takes her arm and almost pulls her to her feet but she shakes off his hand and marches towards the door knocking into a neighbouring table: tinkling of glass; murmurs of protest. Baudoin follows her with outstretched fingers just touching her elbow, but even this tenuous contact is broken as she pushes through the revolving door, leaving him to execute an awkward little jig in order to fit himself into the next whirling segment. He catches her at the news kiosk and turns her around to face him, but is distracted by the waiter who has followed him onto the street – '*Forty francs, monsieur, service compris.*' Baudoin releases Gabrielle's arm to fish out his wallet and without looking at it thrusts a note into the waiter's hand, but Gabrielle has broken free and is half running, doubly blinded, up the street in the wrong direction. She almost collides with a little old lady in a black straw hat with red cherries on its brim, and disappears in the crowd.

'So what was it all about?' Madame Genet asked, licking the tip of her pencil and adding up a column of figures. Old Hautrive wiped out the last of the ashtrays and critically eyed the racks of polished glasses. 'The usual thing. She knows about the other woman. He denies it; claims he's under pressure at the office. She hasn't seen him for days, accuses him of sneaking about in disguises because the other woman has a jealous husband.'

'I've never heard that one before.'

Hautrive tossed his white coat into the pile with the others and reached for his suit jacket. 'Just a variation on an old theme,' he said. '*Plus ça change, plus c'est la même chose.*'

5

One evening towards the end of March, Baudoin received an unexpected visit from *maître* Alain Claudel, the husband of Gabrielle's best friend, Marie Jeanne. Baudoin had no affection for the man and understood even less the attraction between the two women. They typified everything that was narrowly stuffy in Gabrielle's bourgeois upbringing.

'Excuse me for dropping in like this,' said Claudel, peeling off his gloves and stuffing them into his overcoat pocket. 'I was just passing and thought I'd look in.' Which was a transparent lie: no one of Claudel's caste ever 'dropped in' on anyone. He turned and shook hands with a smile of practised cordiality belied by the distant appraisal in his eyes. Baudoin took his coat and waved him towards the sitting room.

'Let me clear away those papers, Alain.'

Claudel examined the settee and then sat down in it, crossing one leg over the other and surveying the clutter in the room with barely concealed distaste. He was clearly ill at ease and didn't know how to begin.

'How is Gabrielle?' The question hung in the air as he patted his pockets for his cigarette case to bridge the awkward pause.

'Marie Jeanne has obviously put you up to this,' thought Baudoin. 'She's well, I think . . . a whiskey? I'm sorry but there's no ice.'

Claudel accepted the drink, examined it as if the glass might be dirty and then rearranged his features into a semblance of masculine bonhomie. 'We haven't seen you for some time,' he said. 'We miss our little bridge evenings.'
'Another lie,' thought Baudoin. Gabrielle has been crying on Marie Jeanne's shoulder for the past three weeks. As for the 'little bridge evenings', they had, in fact, been disastrous. The same charming impulsiveness and improvisation that made Gabrielle a delightful companion were misplaced in a bridge partner. She bid like a drunken Maharajah at Monte Carlo. Marie Jeanne was indulgent; Claudel, who played with maddening precision, was hypocritically polite; and Baudoin, who had made efforts to please Gabrielle, was by turns bad tempered or transparently bored and, towards the end, increasingly preoccupied, falling into reveries in the middle of a hand.

'Let me get you a clean ashtray, Alain,' said Baudoin getting up, wishing that Claudel would stop beating about the bush. He almost tripped over Ludmilla the cat, who had picked that exact moment to spring out from under a chair, stalking what appeared to be a catnip mouse, but which was in reality Baudoin's greying walrus moustache. Baudoin just missed retrieving it before Ludmilla pounced again, batting it across the room to land at Claudel's feet. He picked it up gingerly between finger and thumb, as one might a dead sparrow, shot a quick glance at Baudoin's upper lip, and deposited it beside the lamp. Baudoin turned his back and almost choked on a large gulp of whiskey, experiencing a sudden vision, from Claudel's perspective, of his moustache abandoning the humdrum security under Baudoin's nose to lead an independent life: wander around the apartment in search of adventure – join the Legion, run away to sea. Most of this was doubtless the result of too much whiskey on an empty stomach, but Baudoin's shoulders were now shaking dangerously and he crossed to the relative shadow near the windows where he had been standing when the bell rang. He searched furiously for the ashtray and emptied it noisily into the wastepaper basket, trying to prevent, while at the same time wishing to surrender completely, gloriously, to an attack of insane laughter that he could feel mounting from his solar plexus. He peered out of the window with tears streaming from his eyes and saw, through shimmering eyelashes, a light turned on in the bedroom across the street. Quite forgetting about Claudel, he tried to visualise the old woman in her bedroom. He saw a book picked up from the night table and tried to read the title but it would not come into focus, then slippered feet crossing the carpet to the bathroom and a heavily veined hand groping in the medicine cabinet for a sleeping pill. The light went out.

'Earlier than usual,' he murmured aloud to himself.
'I beg your pardon?' said Claudel.
Who had spoken? Ah yes, Claudel, the troublesome busybody. "The buds – the buds on the trees – spring!' said Baudoin, and then somewhat belligerently: 'Listen, Alain, I don't know why Gabrielle has involved you in all this. Perhaps Marie Jeanne, who has undoubtedly told you all about it, imagines that I will unburden myself to another man. As usual, the truth is completely banal . . . in spite of Gabrielle's absurd fantasies, there simply isn't "another woman". You know how Gabrielle is; she's not been getting enough

attention lately and can think of no reason other than that there's a *femme fatale* lurking somewhere.'

Baudoin was by this time pacing the floor, irritated at having to explain himself. He stopped to push a medical dictionary under a chair with his foot and noticed that he had been gesticulating with the ashtray still in his hand – which irritated him even more.

'I've been more than ever preoccupied with a research project for the office, that's all, and have less time for Gabrielle at the moment. I don't know why I'm telling you all this' – it's none of your business you blundering fool – 'except that you may be able to convince her it's all nonsense.' Claudel's eyes strayed to the binoculars mounted on the tripod by the window which Baudoin had forgotten to dispose of when he answered the door.

'Let me get you another drink, Alain,' said Baudoin, finally delivering the ashtray. 'He thinks I'm mad,' he thought, picking up Claudel's glass. 'Actually, of course, there is another woman . . . but she's seventy years old.' And he almost started to giggle again.

6

It was getting warm enough to sit out in the Jardin du Luxembourg. Workmen were setting out the miniature trees in their green wooden tubs, returned from wherever they'd disappeared to during the colder months. A slight overcast softens contrast, heightening the vermilion and violet of geranium and lobelia to a heartbreaking intensity, which is carried to the eye (as the Impressionists knew) through the medium of translucent, almost palpable, Parisian air. Their hues might have been selected from some Fauvist's palette to complement the pale-green painted iron chairs which encircle an octagonal pond, placed just out of range of any wind-blown spray from the dancing fountain in its centre. To the right, upper storeys of grey-blue apartment buildings are just visible above the tops of olive-green, feathery trees lining a long alley leading away towards Montparnasse. Scattered about the lawns or perched on stone balustrades which border the walls, antique Romans and faceless Greeks gesture toward the grass, the sky, the past, the children playing at their feet; indicate the flower beds, or inwardly ruminate past glory and the unpredictable ways of gods and men. In the distance, wearing that abstracted expression common to his fraternity, a solitary runner glides silently under the trees in lonely communion with his aching thighs. Splotches of diffused sunlight camouflage his tricolor track suit. A small boy in white stockings with a skinned knee leans far out over the pond's low parapet and its dazzling water to retrieve, with an inadequate stick, a red, white and blue sail boat left over from some Dufy sketch. The ping and plonk of tennis comes from somewhere close behind.

Nearby, not far from the boy in white stockings, sits an elderly woman dressed in inappropriately sombre black. She watches the boy, smiles to herself and returns to the book which lies open upon her lap.

Further along, almost halfway round the circle of pale-green chairs, sits a workman in a beret and blue overalls who has brought his lunch from a nearby building site in a black tin box. He munches a sandwich and squints at *Le Figaro* through heavily rimmed spectacles. There is something indefinably wrong about his appearance. Perhaps he should be reading *Combat* instead of *Le Figaro*; the hand which holds the sandwich is not blunt fingered and roughened by manual labour; the fingernails are too clean, the heavy work shoes too new.

The Boulevard St Michel. A pretty German girl (clear skin, blonde hair cut short for swimming); in the pocket of her blue jeans is a crumpled letter from the Faculté de Sciences Politiques terminating her scholarship and an irate note from her father commanding her to return home immediately. She accosts an obvious countryman whom she has observed for several minutes strolling aimlessly up and down the pavement. He wears a grey-green alpine hat, loden coat, carries a knobbly walking stick and a German language guide to Paris. A brief conversation ensues. The gentleman replies in French (to show off his accent, she supposes). He smiles confusedly, regrets, suddenly sees something further down the street which engages his attention and hastily departs, shrugging apologetically.

Two days later the same tourist, this time wearing dark glasses and carrying the morning edition of *Der Spiegel* astounds a taxi driver at the Carrefour de l'Odéon by commanding him to follow the number twelve bus. His attitude and gesture unconsciously duplicate Danton's – high on his pedestal just behind, whose outstretched bronze arm and pointing forefinger seem to be summoning another taxi, or indicating the way to the Bastille – where the bus is going anyway.

The Jardin du Luxembourg again. The little old lady in black is re-reading Stendhal or knitting a red and black muffler – an unimportant detail. The boy in the white stockings has not come today. The workman in blue overalls has been replaced by a North American visitor, possibly from Cincinnati, sitting at three o'clock to the old woman's noon around the circle of green painted chairs. He wears a navy-blue baseball cap, a grey athletic shirt and corduroys. His eyes are invisible behind mirrored sunglasses. Binoculars dangling from a leather strap around his neck proclaim the overly conscientious tourist or perhaps a misguided bird-watcher who would do better in the forest of Fontainebleau or even the Bois de Vincennes, if that is really his game, for he ignores what must be a handbook to European birds (or a guide to the gardens) lying open on the seat beside him, but finds plenty of time to ogle passing girls – students mostly, hugging heavy books to softly yielding tee-shirt fronts and parading Gabrielle's sleek buttocks, tightly encased in blue denim, past his frankly longing gaze. The tourist tears his eyes away and looks over towards the little old lady who is reflected for an instant in his glasses as a tiny black spot amidst a riot of green, vermilion, violet and blue – and beyond her, towards the shaded alley of the goldfish pond near the sentry box at the side entrance to the Senate (where a blue-shirted soldier of the *Garde Républicaine* is going quietly insane). Impossible to say whether the pond actually contained goldfish. Earlier in the week he thought he had seen dull orange moving in the murky black and wondered whether they were fed by some municipal employee or left to fend for themselves. There was little else to look at except the preposterous sculpture at the end of the pond . . . there beyond where she was sitting, still knitting: a nineteenth-century romantic's conception of a woodland nymph or muse lying nude across the knees of some Apollo or other. Her provocative posture, naked thighs and sculpted belly evoked images of Gabrielle in one of her more abandoned moods – reawakening insistent pangs he thought subdued. Mad, impetuous Gabrielle who had once greeted him at the door (first peeking carefully round it) clad only in a gauze curtain removed from one of the front windows – the entire apartment ablaze with the lascivious glimmering of half a hundred black candles, *black* candles, erect and shimmering in every candelabra, candlestick, saucer, and plate, filling the rooms with a tropical warmth to match the burning incense – spirals of white smoke rising, perspiration's sheen on a white shoulder seen in enormous close up . . . Another pair of shoulders, suntanned these, and glistening slightly from the fountain's windblown spray, passed by filling the tourist's field of vision. All these impressions merged for Baudoin into a gentle blur of colour and movement from which the old woman's frail black figure would suddenly leap out in sharp focus – silhouetted against the limestone façade of the Comédie Française as she slowly climbed the worn stone steps toward the shady side-galleries leading to the gardens or stepping carefully off the curb at the end of a familiar street – stirring recollections for Baudoin of an earlier time – remembered scenes and fragmentary vistas not recalled since his student days, nor revisited, although this quarter was within a short distance of his apartment. He quite enjoyed the walks, sometimes felt quite happy, as if he were engaged in the most normal activity in the world, at other times could not recall how he came to be following an elderly woman around in the street instead of one of the younger ones in well-filled blue jeans that he kept encountering – that pretty German girl for instance. He smiled ruefully to himself and hesitated at the corner. The old woman had stopped in front of a florist's window and seemed on the point of going in. Baudoin exchanged glances with a Persian cat sitting in a bookshop window among dusty aboriginal gewgaws and Zulu wedding finery. From his right came the roar of an expresso machine and the bop-, bop-, bop-, click, bop ratata ping! of a pinball machine being manhandled in a student cafe. A wheezing and bowlegged white terrier hobbled past on tender feet.

It would have been difficult for Baudoin to say what his hopes and intentions were. Was it merely curiosity or did he have some specific aim in view? Did he hope to deduce how much longer she might continue to live from the strength or lack of it which she displayed climbing the steps of the Comédie Française (God knows she got around enough). Did he hope to see her stagger suddenly and clutch her heart? Would he have contemplated a tiny push as she stood on a narrow pavement inches from speeding traffic . . . seize her and bend her backwards over the fountain's parapet – a single silvery bubble escaping from between compressed grey lips, blue-veined pale claw clutching convulsively at his clip-on bow tie, snatching off his bowler hat and unsettling his blond wig, dentures expelled by a sudden rush of bubbles sliding in silent finality to the bottom and coming to rest beside a dully glinting ten-franc piece lost by some boy yachtsman? No. His hopes and intentions were as unclear to him now as they had been since he had signed that damnable contract and begun to watch his small inheritance from Aunt Berthe being all too rapidly eaten away.

Madame Vallette changed her mind and walked back towards the florist's, passing on the way a devout priest in a long black cassock whose nose was almost buried in his breviary. Surely that was the same visiting priest she'd seen at Mass last Sunday.

7

During the months that followed, Baudoin's curiosity about the old woman across the street was to assume the proportions of an obsession: he could predict with considerable accuracy her shopping list, knew how often she visited the hairdresser in the rue du Dragon and how long she stayed there, knew her doctor's name and had even been inside his waiting room (although he had stopped short of posing as a patient in the hope, somehow, of rifling the card file). He kept notes and timetables of her movements and even those of her domestic (who lived in Billancourt, arrived by the number forty bus and was in the habit of going to the cinema every Thursday after finishing work). His preoccupation took up almost all of his waking hours, and some of his sleeping ones. Nothing had been cleaned or tidied in the apartment since his quarrel with Gabrielle (door keys left lying under the mat, two or three rattling coat hangers in the bedroom *armoire*). A thin film of cigarette ash covered everything, as if Vesuvius were just outside the window, and he stalked from room to room muttering to himself amidst an untidy clutter of experimental false noses, wigs, diagrams, actuarial statistics, unopened letters, and abandoned items of costume. Quick-change dickies, colourful clip-on cravats and wilted bows, resembling bedraggled moths in some provincial museum's collection, crept out of bureau drawers and overflowed onto the floor. Ramshackle tam o'shanters, dusty bowlers and forest-green alpine hats occupied chairs or squatted on the floor. An empty flower vase wore a blond wig. If the telephone rang (which it did less and less frequently), it did so with a querulous, faraway tone from under a pile of yellowing newspapers and neglected correspondence, obliging him to root around in a month's accumulated neglect in order to put a stop to its complaining. Unpaid bills lay in scattered piles – from under which he sometimes thought he heard rustling, like small animals moving under dead leaves. Overdue library books (mostly medical reference works) stared at him reproachfully from the bedside table whenever he went into the bedroom. A smell of neglect, as if from a decaying Venetian palazzo, pervaded the atmosphere. One could almost hear stagnant canal water lapping under the floor boards.

Absurd! What a bizarre notion! . . . like that incident the day before yesterday, hurrying up the boulevard towards the market in the rue de Buci; inadvertently somehow falling into step with a man wearing an identical hat and black raincoat, so that for an instant one experienced the uncanny sensation of walking beside one's own reflection in a mirror. Outdoors! In broad daylight! Or that damned ventilator on the rooftop across the street which, when looked at obliquely, resembled a man peeping round a chimney watching the windows. Baudoin ridiculed the notion to himself, but nevertheless could not avoid a tiny start each time he caught it out of the corner of his eye . . . looked at directly, of course, it reassumed the guise of a harmless ventilator. Baudoin did not identify with these fancies . . . did not actually believe that there were men watching him from the roof tops: he was more bemused than alarmed by his eye's whimsical aberrations; in respect to his body he had become an impartial, not unsympathetic, bystander. He observed, for instance, that he seemed to have forgotten how to perform all kinds of simple automatic movements . . . how much pressure was required to open or close a cupboard door for example and noted with interest that he had twisted a knob off again. It did not amuse him nor on the other hand unduly alarm him when his finger pressed the wrong button in the lift – delivering him to doors which his key did not open; that his cigarette had been lit in the middle, or that his foot had misjudged the height of the curb, causing him to stagger in the street once again for no apparent reason.

More disquieting was the suspicion that the reverse might also be true . . . that his body had developed a certain independence in respect to himself – an indifference to his fate so to speak. It had begun to cavil, demur, reminding him with the odd twinge, small rebellions in the joints, a mulish sulking in the stomach, or an infrequent but ominous suspicion of syncopation in the regular rhythm of his heartbeat, that unqualified cooperation could no longer be taken for granted. This indifference, moreover, seemed to have seeped into the atmosphere of his surroundings – his apartment. He sensed disapproval shading into malevolent mischievousness lurking in the hallways – as if his apartment rejected him as a *locataire*. Objects were frivolously unsympathetic or downright unfriendly: the claw and ball feet of this or that dresser or commode seemed poised equally for a playful game of bowls or to launch missiles at his head. Things went haywire, fell apart perversely. At the same time that his back started to play up, the leg fell off the settee. Upholstery grew tufts like hairy ears and the carpet, in mimicry of his own, began to display incipient bald spots. The front door catch developed a negligent looseness: draughts would open it unbidden like a phantom butler forever ushering in guests who were never there. The electric clock had out of sheer pique committed suicide – suffered a spasm and whirled its hands around faster and faster till they flew off and fell to the bottom of the case with a tiny, tinny tinkle. Veneer peeled from his favourite wardrobe which now resembled a derelict *clochard* in a loose mahogany mackintosh about to let drop the last polished panel, revealing its knotty knees; from time to time he caught it leering at him lewdly as if he were a pretty girl in the park. The kitchen cabinet had developed a mysterious list to port, so that an egg or an onion, when set down, tended to roll away mischievously and jump to the tiles. Floorboards in the WC creaked ominously and seemed to have settled by several inches so that one walked uphill to the kitchen and downhill to the bathroom. (He knew that one day he would pull the chain and fall enthroned into the apartment below; imagined the undertaker, unable to find him under all that lath and plaster, burying the lot, toilet and all, in an enormous packing case.) The left sleeve of the black cardigan which he wore in lieu of a dressing-gown had begun to unravel, leaving a complicated trail of black yarn (curiously resembling the diagrams he had made of the old woman's movements about the neighbourhood) from bedroom, to bathroom, to kitchen to sitting room. Every now and then he would retrace this intricate pattern, rolling up the yarn into a neat ball as he went, meticulously going back over his movements in the exact reverse order to avoid becoming hopelessly ensnarled at the intersections. If he started, say, at 9 p.m. in the sitting room, he could follow his movements back to 10 a.m. in the bedroom, ending up with the day in a nice, neat ball of yarn – except that the sleeve of his cardigan had grown several inches shorter. Forcing the metaphor, Baudoin began to wonder if he couldn't trace every association, every memory, back into the past and arrive ultimately at infancy with his entire life wound up in a tidy little ball. Maybe then he could find those places where its orderly progress had become snarled; discover where the buffoonery of a careless and indifferent fate, by tiny increments of aberration – dropped stitches, missed rows – had allowed his life to transform itself into, say, a fourteen-foot muffler or some whale's cardigan.

Perhaps the process had already unconsciously begun. Maybe that was the explanation for his recent bout of total recall . . . images of the past that popped at random into his head at any time of day in no matter what circumstances: a cloud's shadow racing towards him over wheat fields at tremendous speed, like the shock wave from a silent explosion; this image seen from a train window (but in what country, and what year, and what was the reason for the journey?); a gigantic oak tree standing at the side of an anonymous brick-paved road; a white wall evoking a green lawn and a small boy . . . two green slatted chairs flanking the flat red oval of a garden table; on the table a solitary empty glass.

He was at least relatively certain that these images came from his own memory, but lately he had begun to entertain the notion that he was tuned in to someone else's. He knew that such a thing was possible with the telephone . . . he used to dial Gabrielle's number only to find himself listening to a conversation between two businessmen discussing share prices. Always the same two, one with a vague hint of Midi accent. Baudoin had tried to join the conversations with improvised stock quotations and spurious buy and sell orders but somehow never seemed to make his voice heard.

Baudoin shifted his position in the bed and half-opened his eyes, slowly bringing into focus the wallpaper's ornamental curlicues echoing the whorls and loops of a signature which, in the dream just ended, he had been affixing to a mountain of documents, taking them from a towering stack on his left and signing his name over and over again in a hand that bore no resemblance to his own – a madman's signature adorned with squiggles, claws, bombastic flourishes. The pen worked only intermittently or not at all, obliging him to sign the same copy several times or laboriously retrace missing letters to match up with the others.

He lay there thinking this over, following with his eyes the windings and turnings of the stylised tendrils and stems climbing towards the ceiling, the rambling motif here and there abruptly interrupted, where a careless paper-hanger had failed to match the pattern. The resulting, somehow disquieting, displacement echoed visually a lingering mood of *non sequitur* left over from another section of the dream, already fading from his memory, in which he seemed to be planning a journey to a destination lying always just beyond the margin of a map. In this blank, indifferent margin, this no man's land, occurred derailments and missed connections. Nothing followed on: roads that stopped abruptly at the edge (promising greener fields, more picturesque villages, blue foothills fading to lighter blue mountains) were not continued in the next section. Sudden roads leading to other towns and villages started arbitrarily anywhere and shot off in any old direction. Rivers that did not exist on, say, section A-23 could be seen gurgling merrily away in section A-24, echoing from the walls of southern gorges, sliding past slag heaps or through mill races at the foot of retired and stationary mill wheels; a barge or two: bright paintwork, pansies in the window box and a fox terrier barking at a cyclist on the bridge.

Baudoin threw back the bedclothes and sat up. Outside the window, with an aerialist's bravura disregard for the four-storey drop to the courtyard below, Ludmilla prepared to lunge at a fly slowly climbing the window pane. He swung his feet to the floor, lit a cigarette, and getting one toe hooked into a slipper that had tried to crawl away under the bed, padded wearily into the bathroom. Balancing the cigarette on the edge of the basin next to a rusty razor blade, he began to soap the bluish jowls of a puffy-eyed individual, somewhat resembling himself, who gazed back dubiously from the mirror. The unfamiliar patch of bristle just under the nose where his moustache used to be felt scratchy to the touch. He had never quite reconciled himself to his facial nudity after the amputation; the faces he made while bringing his razor to bear in the difficult angles under the nostrils seemed distinctly alien. Madam Q., his concierge, among others, had remarked on its absence – commented at length as he fidgeted where she trapped him on the landing, pretending that it took years off his appearance and no doubt making some connection with Mademoiselle Gabrielle's almost simultaneous disappearance. He had to smile (as best he could with his upper lip pulled down in a lugubrious moue) remembering the narrowly averted catastrophe one evening as he encountered her at the entrance having by some unaccountable lapse forgotten to remove the grizzled *schnurbart* which he had just taken for a trial run down the boulevard. A simulated sneeze – handkerchief clapped over his face in the nick of time as he rushed past her to the stairs – had prevented her seeing the sudden, miraculously sprouted adornment occupying what should have been a blank under his nose.

He splashed water on his face (extinguishing the cigarette which hissed and went out), trying to remember what day it was. There was something he had to do, but for the moment couldn't recall what it was. He towelled his face, or what was left of it, and trailing a thin worm of black yarn behind him, padded silently down the hall to the sitting room.

On the writing desk was a sheet of note paper: at the top: 'Chérie' and then 'chère Gabrielle', finally 'Gabrielle chérie', under that three or four sentences crossed out, started again and again crossed out. He lit another cigarette, staring blankly at an overdue service report for his firm which had been lying there unfinished for a week or more and then withdrew from a stuffed pigeon-hole a three- or four-page document bound together with blue ribbon which he read for perhaps the fourth or fifth time: '. . . and to continue thus quarter by quarter until the decease of Madame Honorine Vallette, vendor, at which time the said rent shall be redeemed and amortised.' He stuffed the document back in the pigeon-hole and began to flip through the pages of a dog-eared pocket-sized notebook which opened to a page whose corner had been bent over as if to mark the place: 'Key' it began, and then '1. old woman's handbag, 2. concierge's duplicate, 3. maid's key.' The first two items had been crossed out. Under 'maid's key' were the words 'Handbag – Thursdays – Cinema.' Baudoin picked up a pencil, chewed the tip meditatively, tapped it idly on the desk top, producing a satisfyingly incisive series of clicks, then underlined the last three words: *'Handbag, Thursdays, Cinema.'* At his feet lay a calendar which had fallen to the carpet: 'UIN' it said (the J having been doodled over in black pencil to match the surround). Crescents or full white discs on some squares indicated the phases of the moon (for whose benefit he had never been able to discover – excepting, possibly, worried administrators of lunatic asylums). One date had been heavily circled in the same black pencil: Thursday, the fifth of June. Baudoin stubbed out his cigarette, got up and crossed to the windows.

8

Monday he had an appointment with his boss. The panelled, soundproof door clicked shut discreetly and Lacaussade came round his desk to take Baudoin's hand in both of his. They were muscular and suntanned. The gold band of his diamond ring felt cold to the touch. He wore an arctic blue shirt, crisp and cool as an iceberg, matching perfectly the colour and temperature of his penetrating, intelligent eyes, a Dior silk tie, and luxuriously gleaming brogues the colour of old teak that might have been hung for years between the breasts of negresses to give them that antique patina. He bestowed on Baudoin his most avuncular – an almost tender – smile, gave his hand the tiniest terminal squeeze and indicated a chair.

Massive was the word for Lacaussade – massive and magisterial. Whether leaning relaxed and assured with one tweedy elbow on the oak mantelpiece a negligent inch from his pale silver riding trophies, or erect behind his baronial desk, as he was now, he seemed to take up more space than ordinary people, leaving his visitors with a vaguely claustrophobic sensation, as if they'd been locked in with a lion . . . a kindly, even jovial lion, but a lion nevertheless. His office was appropriately spacious – necessarily spacious to accommodate this leonine man with the silvery mane and so much animal energy – and because Lacaussade never did anything in a small way; what he did, moreover, he did with savoir faire, easy assurance and impeccable, if perhaps slightly flamboyant, good taste. He had an apartment in the Parc Monceau (now occupied by his ex-wife), a house near Mont Morency, a summer villa in Bagur on the Costa Brava and a garçonnière in one of the Latin Quarter's more fashionable squares. He rode, swam, climbed, played tennis, billiards and bridge, shot golf in the eighties, collected two-hundred-year-old Sèvres and girls of eighteen. He was vice-president in charge of sales of Montbrun Tissandier and his surroundings reflected his status: over the fireplace hung a Cézanne – a little-known view of the Mont St Victoire inherited, people said, from his first wife. On the floor was an enormous, whitely gleaming polar bear rug . . . a homesick polar bear with ruby gums, and ivory fangs, wearing a snappy red felt lining on his underside, who languished on the polished parquetry disconsolately listening to the discreet whispers of air conditioning and the soughing of traffic in the Champs Elysees. Upon Lacaussade's panelled walls no mundane sales charts hung; no unsightly sheafs of sales statistics cluttered his antique desk; nor did his regal visage betray the slightest note of worry or concern that one of his best salesmen was cracking up.

    He'd shaved his moustache and lost his girl, that was first. Second, he was going to seed – blue socks with a brown suit, a wilted collar and razor nick under the nose. A certain period of disorientation was normal and permissible after a woman goes (there had been some talk of marriage there, he recalled – some charming girl). He remembered his own depression after moving out of the Parc Monceau, but this showed signs of going on too long. '*Merde! C'est le bouquet.*' (That's all we need.) The next thing you know he'd be caught flashing in the Bois or drinking too much. Lacaussade looked closely at the skin around Baudoin's eyes.

'How are you feeling, René? You should get more exercise, *mon grand* . . . take up tennis or squash. Brisson jogs now, you know – three kilometres a day, twice round the Jardin du Luxembourg every morning. Says it makes him feel ten years younger.' Baudoin shifted nervously in his chair and looked down at the toe of his right shoe which was within three inches of the polar bear's gaping maw. He withdrew his foot hastily and looked about for an ashtray.

'The annual check-up is not obligatory, as you know,' went on Lacaussade, 'but it's an excellent idea. See old Hervieu – so professional and reassuring. He specialises in problems of *comment dirais-je* – how shall I say – the mature male? He's almost a father to me. One moment, René.' Lacaussade punched the intercom with a manicured forefinger and spoke into it. 'Not now, Mademoiselle Mercier, I'll be with you in fifteen minutes . . . *Comment?*' He consulted his old-fashioned gold pocket watch, snapped it shut again, and returned it to his waistcoat pocket. '*Oui . . . oui* . . . I'll be ready on time. Have Robert ready with the car and give him the ticket. *Mais, oui*, Terminal Three . . . *entendu* . . . Robert knows . . . *merci, chérie.*' His intercom smile faded abruptly and he flicked an invisible speck off his sleeve. Baudoin returned from a stroll down the sun-drenched flank of the Mont St Victoire – Mediterranean air heavy with the scent of pine still lingering in his nostrils.

'The reason I wanted to have this little chat, René, is that, frankly, we've been a bit worried about you. I had a call from Bollinger last week and he was positively irate . . . a difficulty with one of the machines which we had to have Hervé take care of.' He picked up a silver and ivory letter opener and weighed it in his hand. 'Bollinger seems to feel he's being neglected. We've smoothed it all over now but I suggest you have a drink with him, reassure the man. After all, Delaroche Borel is an important client.' He paused for a second to let that one register. The polar bear rolled his eyes upward toward Baudoin; they shone with understanding and compassion. 'I've decided to let in a little fresh air,' Lacaussade continued, '. . . give Hervé a crack at it. The big boys are important but we mustn't forget the smaller ones that put us in business. Some of them are getting restless and need to see a familiar face from time to time . . . a handsome face like yours, René.' Lacaussade smiled at his own little joke and reached for his briefcase. 'Give me a little review of your ideas for next year with special attention to D.D.S.M. and Michaelson' (he pronounced Michaelson with an American accent). 'If you need any advice I'm always available. Cheer up, René. Buy yourself a new suit. I could give you my tailor's name in the rue St Florentin. He's an absolute artist.'

Lacaussade stood up and took Baudoin's hand, bestowed once more his famous smile and was already reaching for the intercom. Baudoin went towards the door, being careful not to step on the polar bear rug.

9

Thursday the fifth of June. If the girl was going where he thought she was going, Baudoin wanted to be close behind her. She cut diagonally across the street in the driving rain and he darted after her causing a driver to swear as he braked suddenly on the wet pavement. Baudoin squeezed between two parked cars, smearing his raincoat and begriming one hand which he wiped with a handkerchief as he ran. He remembered only one cinema in the immediate vicinity – one of those small studios dedicated to revivals of classic films. Sure enough, she turned right at the corner and headed in that direction. He was next in line at the ticket window but almost passed her in the tiny lobby where she stopped to buy sweets – resting the handbag on the counter as she withdrew her coin purse. Baudoin shook the rain from his black slouch hat and studied stills of coming attractions.

His later recollection combined three distinct sets of impressions: the event as he had imagined it, as it actually happened, and as he remembered it. There were some points of correspondence: her bare legs silhouetted against the moving circle of light thrown upon the carpet by the usherette's torch was exactly as he had seen it in his mind's eye, but his imagination, which was more visual than olfactory, had not supplied the odour of damp wool in the close atmosphere of the cinema, nor the whiff of garlic mingled with her cheap scent as he surrendered his ticket to the usherette and took the next seat but one in the almost empty row. Luck. Sheer luck. He sat back in the welcome, anonymous darkness, grateful for a brief postponement. What now? Sheer momentum had carried him this far, but now he faced the unavoidable moment. It was always at this point in his imagined rehearsals – as in a recurrent nightmare where one desperately tries to redirect the chain of images leading to an undefined but certain terror lurking up some back alley of the mind – that Baudoin compulsively reconsidered alternative stratagems for obtaining a key to the old woman's apartment. To steal a duplicate (assuming that there was one) from the rack in the concierge's lodge was too risky, if not impossible; if he managed to snatch the old woman's bag in the street or a crowded market without being recognised or caught (nightmares of running through a crowd pursued by outraged passers-by) she would, in all probability, merely have her locks changed. On the other hand, he could not be sure that the girl two seats away on the aisle even had an extra key, or that she was carrying it now. He had seen her arrive for work at the flat across the street when he knew her employer to be out, but she might have been let in by the concierge or borrowed her duplicate. He forced himself to concentrate: 'Exit' glared red over a doorway to the left of the screen and he tried to visualise the street it gave onto – or did it lead back through a corridor towards the entrance? A second door next to the exit was identified by the illuminated silhouette of an Edwardian dandy tipping his hat and he was suddenly aware of an urgent need. His legs were cramped and uncomfortable in a seat that must have been designed for midgets. Somewhere behind him a sweet paper crackled. On the screen directly in front of him, the thug's negroid face zoomed up enormously – every pore and acne scar sharply defined in the oblique light of a street lamp. He dragged deeply on a cigarette cupped in his palm against the downpour and then flicked it away. Baudoin badly wanted to smoke. He glanced sideways at the girl and dimly perceived the handbag resting between her thigh and the armrest. Both of her hands were occupied with a box of sweets. The villain, with nightmarish synchronism, was now stalking the girl down twisting back streets. His grotesquely enlarged shadow followed, sliding silently past on the wall, slipping in and out of doorways. The girl hears another set of footfalls echoing her own, pauses to listen; the footsteps also stop. She ducks abruptly into a narrow passageway which betrays her by terminating in a blank wall . . . heart beating wildly she turns to confront her pursuer, just as Baudoin, heart thumping in synchronisation with the sound track, decided to make his move.

'*Pardon, Mademoiselle, je m'excuse.*' Halfway past her into the aisle he pretended to lose his balance and thrust out a hand to keep from toppling into her lap. She must have thrown up her arm to ward him off because the bag came into his hand without resistance. He was halfway down the aisle toward the exit, with a dim impression of spilled bonbons crunching underfoot, before she could recover. The rising note of an outraged female voice superimposed on a scream of terror from the soundtrack was cut off by the swing doors as he scuttled down the stairs to the street. The rain was still falling steadily and no one was there to see him stuff something into an unfolded shopping bag or cram on a beret and dark glasses as he raced towards the nearest corner, expecting to hear a shout or running footsteps behind him (an echo from the soundtrack or his own bad dreams?). His heart thumped loudly and seemed to skip a beat as he rounded the corner, and ducked into a side street, where a stout woman in a fur coat was trying unsuccessfully to shelter under an upheld newspaper as she shifted her bulk out through the narrow back door of a taxi.

Baudoin got out in front of the Rotonde two blocks past his apartment, tipped the driver, and walked straight past the bar to the toilets. A half hour later, somewhat tipsy, he up-ended the handbag onto his dining table. Feminine odds and ends cascaded onto its polished surface: a crumpled white handkerchief, scented with her perfume, unpleasantly evoking the cramped darkness of the cinema, an atomiser of the stuff which rolled onto the floor, a battered address book between cheap cardboard covers, coin purse, black plastic rosary beads, and yes . . . three, no four, key-rings! (He had forgotten that she must clean for more than one little old lady): an embarrassment of key-rings; a surplus of little old ladies. He was momentarily dismayed. How did she keep track of so many keys – and why did she carry all of them? One bunch appeared to be identified by a strip of soiled surgical tape folded over through the ring to make an improvised tag; another had a small, round cardboard disc attached by a loop of string; two were smugly incognito. The tape yielded 'Obrein' or 'Obrium' in smudged pencil, probably misspelled; on the tag was merely 'Sra. V.'. Sra. V – he picked up the address book, whose cover proclaimed it to be the property of

Concepta Martinez, and remembered a trace of Spanish or Portuguese accent when she had bought her ticket. He thumbed through to the V's. There it was at the bottom of the third page: Señora V. – tel. LIT 1463. LIT was his own exchange and almost certainly the old woman's.

Señora V. – Madame Vallette.

10

Docteur Gamelin transferred the empty physician's bag to his other hand and glanced at his wristwatch . . . surely the light would never change. He adjusted his black homburg and stroked his moustache nervously with a gloved hand – obviously an overworked general practitioner with very little time for house calls. He patted his pocket again and heard the reassuring chink of keys. The light changed at last. He crossed the street quickly and turned west past the terrace of the Deux Magots. The old woman was at the hairdresser in the rue du Dragon and would be there for the next hour and a half, unless she had forgotten something or changed her mind and returned unexpectedly while he was descending to the street and donning his disguise piecemeal in various doorways on his roundabout route to the entry of number 180.

He crossed the resounding marble flags to the lift and punched the button professionally as if expecting it to say ouch; the lift merely groaned and began its descent. Unoccupied. No need to take the stairs. He hefted the black bag and glanced at his watch once again for the benefit of the concierge should she be idling in her office behind him. Peering upward through the grillwork he could see the looped lift cable snaking away into the gloom overhead.

The outer door on the fourth floor clanked loudly and he swore silently, then stood listening for a moment before descending the carpeted stairway winding round the lift cage to the landing below. Momentarily disorientated, he had to construct a mental picture of the building's exterior before deciding on the left-most of the two anonymous doors – then dropped his silver pencil to the carpet with the idea of pretending to search for it if surprised on the landing, and, spine crawling in anticipation of danger from the rear, strained to distinguish, through interference of noise on his side of the door, any sound – a radio turned on, door closing, rattle of dishes in the sink – that would betray her presence within. A snatch of conversation from the courtyard below filtered in through the open window; somewhere in the apartment above a door banged; the plumbing groaned passionately as someone turned a tap, ascended to a contralto warble and culminated in an ecstatic squeak. A cat yowled in response. He listened as intently as a condemned man strains to hear the footsteps of the execution party coming to fetch him in the dead of night. For one mad instant he imagined that an eye was peering at him through the peephole in the door and impulsively put his finger over it. His back felt naked, exposed. At any moment he expected the door behind him to open suddenly and prepared to drop to his knees and grope for that pencil. He fought down an almost overpowering impulse to run – retreat swiftly down the stairs and run – forget the whole mad business. Willing his hand into the movement he rang the bell and waited. Gossip in the courtyard continued; the plumbing redescended the octave; cowboys slaughtered Indians somewhere below. Three blocks away an irate motorist honked at a pedestrian; a mile away on the Ile de la Cité, Notre Dame struck four. Baudoin inserted the most likely looking key on the stolen ring; it turned with a satisfyingly smooth movement and he slipped into the apartment, closed the door silently behind him and, exhausted by the effort, stood back against it with his hand still on the knob. Now he was committed.

He listened intently for a cough, the sound of a page being turned, water running in the bath behind a closed door, the dull swish of footfall on the carpet, the sharper scrape of shoe leather on tile. Nothing. Traffic noises in the street below and the ticking of the clock merely heightened the relative silence. Still alert, he gazed about him trying to relate what he could see to his mental floor plan. Directly ahead was a stairway leading to the bedroom and bath, a dripping tap on his left indicated the kitchen, to his right afternoon sun poured through wide glass doors leading to the dining room and *salon*. Suddenly from that direction he heard the soft crackle of a newspaper followed by a thump – and was instantly out of the door and running in panic down the stairs. (Baudoin was halfway down the stairs; his body was still rooted paralysed to the doormat.) He almost sobbed with relief when a grey Persian cat strolled into the *entrée*, stretched luxuriously, gripping the carpet with its claws, then sat down and looked him over. The total boredom of the cat's demeanour, its utter domestic banality, above all its incurious acceptance of his presence, momentarily dispelled Baudoin's anxiety, which gave way to an exhilarating sense of adventure, the sort of emotion felt by a schoolboy left on his own over a weekend exploring forbidden rooms. He went past the cat through the doors into the dining room. On the sideboard, fatally stabbed by two stainless steel knitting needles, a ball of yarn expired quietly bleeding a trickle of red wool onto the mahogany. A copy of *France Soir*, upon which the cat had been napping, lay upon the settee. Fresh violets swam in a white bowl in the centre of a massive oak table. He ran his fingertips over its surface as he moved past it to another set of glazed doors giving onto the salon. On the mantel above the fireplace was a framed photo of graduating young naval cadets, a strangely modern looking snap of Madame Vallette herself as a young bride, and a formal portrait of her husband in naval uniform – moustachioed, competent, unimaginative – who gazed mildly into the room where, for the edification of dinner guests and occasional house breakers, elbowing each other on small tables and sideboards, an indiscriminately acquired collection of exotic bric-à-brac – cheap gewgaws evoking foreign ports of call side by side with better pieces – occupied every available surface and competed for wall space. A sheathed samurai sword hung next to a Bokhara embroidery whose stylised burgundy pomegranates smouldered in the slanting rays of the afternoon sun. A French West African fertility goddess with angular features and a protruding abdomen shared a corner with a Chinese cloisonné vase which had somehow survived the journey intact.

Baudoin browsed idly among the exotica; picked up a piece, examined it, carefully replaced it and picked up another, hefted it in his hand, turned it over to examine the underside and put it down again. He sat down brazenly in the armchair, patted its upholstered arms as if appraising its value at auction and gazed proprietorially about him, got up and crossed to a desk between the windows; picked up a sheet of stationery with the start of a letter in longhand. 'Cher Monsieur', it began and left off. He began to open drawers and riffle through papers: a final reminder from Gaz de France, an estimate for some kind of repairs to the family mausoleum, a post card showing a bronco buster at the Calgary Stampede with the usual illegible message on the back. He started when his own name, hand printed on a blue folder, leaped out at him writ as large as on a theatre marquee. It contained Madame Vallette's copy of the agreement whose twin slept in his desk across the way. Prompted by a sudden mood of insane recklessness, Baudoin closed the desk (which he had found open) and positively sauntered back through the dining room, past the cat asleep on a chair in the *entrée*, and into the kitchen where he tried the taps, peered into the refrigerator, opened cupboard doors, noted that Madame would need more tarragon in the near future, that her gas water-heater was the same age and model as his own – even dipped his finger into the sugar bowl on the table and licked it. Did he think of stealing a banana from the bowl on the table, pour himself a glass of cognac, rinse and wipe the glass and replace the bottle, carefully turning the label to the same position?

Suddenly aware that the excitement had affected his bladder and padding silently up the stairs in search of the bathroom, which he found to his left just where he remembered it, he relieved himself copiously and luxuriously into the bidet and rinsing it carefully, waved his hands about in the air to dry. To the pale-green jade in the soap dish adhered a solitary silvery hair which he picked up between forefinger and thumb and stuffed in his breast pocket – for what reason he could not have explained. Did he intend to carry it away for scientific analysis . . . start a collection of nail parings for Voodoo manipulation? Underclothes hung on a rack over the bath. He was surprised by the miniature shrivelled tights resembling drying squid in some Mediterranean fishing port, seemingly about the right size for a child of five; he had assumed that older women somehow clung to old-fashioned forms of underwear. A soiled adhesive plaster lay in the wastebasket; a single pink rubber glove lying on the rim of the bath gestured toward an open medicine cabinet displaying the universal assortment of multicoloured boxes and tubes; an elastic bandage fastened with a safety pin, a number of brown and amber plastic cylinders with white plastic tops, and squarish bottles with handwritten labels. Poking with a tentative forefinger those in front to reveal what lay behind, and cursing under his breath the low standard of penmanship in the pharmaceutical profession as he unscrewed the cap of his silver fountain pen, Baudoin began to copy the labels quickly into a small notebook (his watch told him he had been in the apartment for almost a half hour). Deciding on a quick reconnaissance of the other rooms, he restored the notebook to his bag and striding rapidly down the hallway turned the corner into the dimly lit bedroom . . . almost straight into the arms of another man who was just coming out!

Baudoin froze, one part of his mind racing wildly, trying unsuccessfully to encompass the impossibility, another part trying to make his feet move. The moustachioed, black-hatted intruder dropped his burglar's tools and staggered backwards gaping; Baudoin dropped his doctor's bag and staggered backwards out of the doorway: . . . he was staring at his own disguised reflection in the full-length mirror of the open wardrobe. He and his reflection turned and bolted for the stairs – Baudoin could hear someone giggling hysterically as they both ran back to retrieve their black bags and rebolted down the stairs, tripping over the edge of the carpet and almost squashing the cat, who spat and flew into the dining room as Baudoin careened past into the *salon* where he opened the desk as he had found it, ran to the front door, peered out of the peephole, forcing himself to wait and listen, and stepped out. Leaning back through the doorway he tipped his hat to the empty hallway, said '*Au revoir, Madame*' to the cat, peering indignantly round the corner, and flew down the stairs. He slowed to a brisk walk passing the concierge's *loge* and stepped into the street, almost colliding with his reflection who hurried away in the opposite direction.

11

It was over the next fortnight that it became gradually apparent to Baudoin, leafing through his little black notebook and pouring over the pharmaceutical catalogues that littered his desk, or brooding in the armchair by the window, that the widow Vallette had suddenly ceased to go out, simply dropped out of sight. No more shopping expeditions to the rue de Buci – delivery boys, parking their bicycles at the curb, were to be seen going into the building with cartons – no more nice walks in the Jardin du Luxembourg, no visits to the hairdresser, not even Sunday mass. At about that time Concepta also disappeared – failing to arrive as usual on Thursdays – which was doubly strange if the old woman had been taken ill, for that was the time she would be most needed to run errands; or if the old lady had died, then it was her ghost that kept turning the lights on and off in different rooms, staying up till all hours reading in the bedroom. On more than one occasion Baudoin, fully clothed, was awakened by the morning sun still in the armchair where he had fallen asleep the night before.

An anxious week went by, and a second. During the time he could manage away from business appointments, Baudoin often spent the entire day glued to the front windows, running when absolutely necessary back and forth to the WC for fear of missing something. He fed an irate Ludmilla in the sitting-room and confined his shopping to the immediate neighbourhood, rushing pell-mell down the stairs to minimise the interval when her doorway across the street would be out of view. Madame Q., his concierge, was convinced he'd gone completely mad – tearing across the *entrée* to the street door and, minutes later laden with purchases, back to the lift again. Searching out Concepta's address book, he twice dialled the widow's number and listened to the phone ringing across the way with a mixture of dread and anticipation. All he could do if she'd answered was to hang up, but that, at least, would be something. An objective observer, in short, would have compared Baudoin's behaviour to that of a love-lorn schoolboy in the throes of his first romance.

Here we have to introduce a brief montage thrown out by the editor but rescued from the trim-bin by the director and reinserted: medium shot and slow track into Baudoin seated in the Jardin du Luxembourg, natty bow tie, itchy wig, bamboo walking stick, pretending to read *Le Rouge et le Noir* – or was it the sports page of *l'Express*? In the medium distance, past his left shoulder an empty, green-painted iron chair; dissolve to artistic close-up of cauliflower in the rue de Buci, track out to reveal Baudoin thumping melons and pinching tomatoes; exterior, long shot in the rue du Dragon, a figure peers through a hairdresser's window, dolly in and cut to the annoyed expression of Madame Spontini, pinning the last curler in place and giving it a final little pat – when for the second time that week a fairly well-dressed but rumpled pervert with a longish nose, hand upraised to shade the reflection of the art gallery behind him, peers at length through her window, ogling her ladies where they sit all in a row under the driers reading magazines. To this add a close-up of Baudoin, kneeling in a *prie dieu* one Sunday morning close to the confessionals on the west side of the Eglise St Germain. A burst of sunshine traversing the azure robes and vitrified heart of Our Saviour high overhead colours his left hand blue and the tip of his nose bright scarlet. On Tuesday we see him in a white apron, breathing heavily, his ear pressed tightly to the widow's back door, trying to catch his breath after a long climb up the service stairs with the contents of his fridge packed into a carton. In the sounds of dishes being washed and snatches of a surprisingly modern popular tune hummed slightly off key, there was nothing to satisfy his desperate curiosity. Doors, doors, doors: Paris, more than any other, is a city of doors – and gateways – like that high, wrought-iron and gilt one over there guarded by the bored sentry in blue cradling a sub machine gun – where Baudoin has just stopped to consult his notebook – high gateways, massively ornate portals guarded by soldiers; heavily panelled doors under the eyes of concierges which, even during the day when they stand wide open, offering you, grudgingly, glimpses of another, parallel Paris – cobbled, secluded, containing trees, an obsolete communal water tap, and yet more doors – seem to interpose ghosts of their closed-up, night-time selves. Mute, inscrutable doors stand on the landing of every apartment building in the city – arms folded, giving nothing away. They stand for privacy, all these doors.

    Here's another one: Greenish discoloration suggesting a conscientious *femme de ménage* surrounds a discreet brass plaque in its centre panel. '*Médecin*,' it whispers behind its hand, 'guess which?' Baudoin already knew; he'd been there before.

The dried-up receptionist with the untidy chignon and incipient moustache that he remembered from his earlier reconnaissance was now a rather sexy redhead with freckles and a Swedish accent. Momentarily thrown off stride, he garbled slightly the beginning of his carefully rehearsed tale (curtain material, I think she said) about a forgotten package that the widow Vallette had asked him to retrieve. Was he a helpful neighbour this time, or the nephew again? No matter.

The girl looked puzzled. 'When was this exactly, Monsieur?'

Baudoin hesitated, 'Last week sometime . . . she hasn't telephoned?'

'*Non*, Monsieur. We received a note a few days ago saying she would be away indefinitely and asking that her bill be sent.'

'She did say something about visiting Carcassonne,' said Baudoin, thinking fast. 'She was born there, you know – but there was some sort of delay. She's very adventurous for a lady of her age.'

'I could telephone her now,' said the girl, and before Baudoin could protest, reached for the telephone.

'No, that won't be necessary. I'd rather not disturb her for a trifle, I can . . . ' She was already dialling. Why did he have to mention the telephone?

'She may be napping. I'd really rather not . . . ' He could hear the telephone ringing with a faraway buzz and considered bolting for the door; sprawling on the carpet in a dead faint; a sudden amorous advance. Would she scream if he snatched the telephone? Had he given a name?

'Your name, Monsieur?'

'My name, what's my name?' he thought. The telephone went on ringing . . .

'No one at home, Monsieur.'

'Well perhaps she's gone off after all,' he said over-heartily, suppressing a desire to cackle with relief. He was almost tempted to make that amorous advance after all. Groping for the knob behind him, he backed towards the door.

'I'll call in again next week sometime.' But next week he was much too busy.

12

The menu handed deferentially to Baudoin by the head waiter of Calvet's was the only one listing prices. Calvet's is that kind of restaurant. Rémy Bollinger of Delaroche Borel put on his half-glasses and scrutinised his with as much deliberation as he would have a maintenance contract. The evening showed no promise of success. Their conversation, heretofore limited to technical subjects, was going to be hard pressed to encompass a social situation. Bollinger, furthermore, was possessed of a singularly opaque personality, screened by an elaborate façade of constant banter (perhaps concealing something inexpressibly tender) that Baudoin, more than a little reserved himself, had in the past made no particular efforts to penetrate. Baudoin moreover was having more difficulty impersonating himself in his role as sales representative of Montbrun Tissandier than, say, a German tourist, or a lift repairman. The relative advantages of this or that machine over some other model seemed as remote and lacking in interest as another coup d'état in the latest African republic.

Bollinger's expensive new teeth clicked embarrassingly once or twice on the cutlery. He was further irritated by a new-found habit of Baudoin's, which he attributed to shyness, of peering at something near the ceiling just over his, Bollinger's, left shoulder. Conversation faltered; Bollinger redoubled his efforts to amuse.

(Calvet's was and still is situated on the Boulevard St Germain at the corner of the rue du Dragon, and, but for the interposition of a bookshop and a men's boutique, could have occupied the ground floor of Baudoin's own building. It commands an excellent view of the buildings opposite; and it was for this reason that Baudoin, in an overdue gesture towards better client relations, was exceeding his brief – and his expense account – following Lacaussade's advice to take Bollinger 'out for a drink'.)

The light in the bedroom window across the street went out and, after an interval, came on in the *salon*.

Bollinger prattled indomitably on, glasses gleaming in the candlelight. The wavering shadow of Baudoin's wine glass, an iridescent ruby in its middle, oscillated wildly to the silent passage of their discreetly invisible waiter, who seemed to be everywhere and nowhere at the same time. Bollinger was getting the hang of his new teeth; the partridge was excellent and the wine well chosen; conversation turned to general topics. Bollinger recounted an amusing story, provoking genuine laughter from his companion and, sharing his triumph, looked around at the other diners. Altogether, things were going better than could have been expected.

It was over cognac that Baudoin, playing close attention to an anecdote concerning a notorious blonde in the typing pool at Delaroche Borel, failed utterly to notice the light go out in the sitting room.

Outside on the pavement a few minutes later, Bollinger, offering his hand, was just going to thank his host for a very pleasant evening: it had all gone so well up to that point. If the eighty-seven bus had been another two seconds behind schedule Baudoin might have missed it entirely: as it was, he just caught a glimpse of a thin figure in black hurrying out of the entrance across the street to a waiting taxi. Bollinger having turned to see what had attracted his companion's attention and restarting his sentence was left staring stupidly at his still extended hand – from which Baudoin's receding figure fled, sprinting for the cab rank at the corner . . . where an aging and very famous film producer, accompanied by his latest protegée, were just pulling up outside the Brasserie Lipp. Patrons on the terrace were diverted by the sight of two gentlemen, a hand each on her elbows, helping one young woman from the cab – the gentleman on the left doing a little dance of impatience as she slid out displaying a very fine pair of legs. The near-sighted producer, who had Chez Lipp mixed up with another restaurant in New York anyway, and mistaking Baudoin for the doorman, held out an enormous film producer-sized tip. Baudoin snatched the note from his hand and pushing it under the cabby's nose scrambled in and slammed the door.

'Follow that cab!'

'*Ecoutez*, Monsieur, that's something that happens in the cinema.'

'Nevertheless. Hurry or we'll miss the light!'

'Just like in the films.'

'Just like in the films. Go on, the light's changing!'

The other cab was already a considerable distance down the boulevard. They barely made the light.

'Your wife, *Patron*?'

'My grandmother. She has a new boyfriend – a band

leader from Marseilles. The family is understandably upset.'

Baudoin strained forward over the seat, his face illuminated by the dashboard's greenish glow, urging the taxi forward with his body, the noise of the radio somehow interfering with his effort to keep the fast receding tail-lights in view, wondering where a little old lady could be going so late at night and why at this crucial juncture, fate had sent him the only witty taxi driver in Paris. Parisian taxis are much alike and there are a lot of them: if Baudoin hadn't noticed the registration number they might have missed it turning into Boulevard St Michel. They were fairly close behind crossing the bridge but got entangled with some pedestrians at Châtelet and missed the signal while the meter ticked off precious seconds. His driver made good time going up the Boulevard Sébastopol however, and they picked up the other cab just turning into the rue Rambouteau where it pulled up at a sleazy, down-at-heel hotel – one of many that used to grace that neighbourhood.

'Drive right past and stop in that space.'

She was just getting the right change out of her coin purse as they rolled past. Baudoin looked out of the back window in time to see her crossing the pavement, her white hair just catching an echo of the hotel's red neon sign. The street was completely deserted except for a woman in a fur jacket carrying an enormous handbag standing in a doorway a little further on; from that direction came the sound of a juke-box playing American jazz. Baudoin risked a glance through the hotel's curtained glass door but could see nothing except a corner of the reception desk. He walked a little way down the pavement and paused to light a cigarette. The woman in the doorway said something he didn't quite catch as he crossed the narrow street and strolled down past the entrance again. Two *agents de police* turned the corner and came towards him down the walk.

He quickened his pace and passed them. Their arrival had given him the beginnings of an idea.

13

Baudoin examined the strip of Fotomat portraits and found them suitably unflattering. Rejecting the first one, with its dead mackerel's eyes produced by a simultaneous blink as the flash popped, and the last, where he had made a bored face at the lens, he snipped out the middle one which wore a slightly more cynical expression and glued it in the upper corner of a homemade document assembled from parts of an outdated driver's licence, a library card and an old customs document bearing suitable stamps and the usual illegible signature. He slipped the collage behind the clear plastic of a cheap leather wallet and eyed the result. The room clerk wasn't going to get more than a glimpse of it anyway. Pulling his heavy grey raincoat on over the thickness of a bulky tweed jacket, he slipped the wallet into an inside pocket and practised fetching it out and flipping it open with that bored, off-hand gesture he'd seen in the movies. Thick-soled walking shoes resurrected from a box in the wardrobe were a nice touch: he imagined that cops always wore heavy shoes. No hat. They never seemed to be wearing hats when you spotted them on the edge of parades or mingling with the crowd at public ceremonies, staring in every direction except towards the central event. He practised an expression of world-weary cynicism in the hall mirror and let himself out.

Just as there are otherwise perfectly normal people who turn out to have a passion for collecting glass dogs or building models of the Eiffel Tower out of matchsticks, Baudoin discovered that he was deriving a lot of secret pleasure from his brief excursions into the lives of the personages that had first presented themselves to his imagination in the mirror of Pembertin et Petin. He remembered with something akin to nostalgia his terror in the cinema as he rushed towards the door with Concepta's handbag. Just as an actor will fasten on little bits of business, carefully observed mannerisms stolen from unsuspecting strangers or acquaintances to flesh out a characterisation, so Baudoin found himself spending more time (the more delightful by reason of the delicious truancy from his job) than was strictly necessary on the details of his impersonations: he tried smoking a pipe, practised different walks, invented ever more fanciful names to go with this or that disguise. On more than one occasion he had extended his surveillance of the old woman beyond its ostensible purpose (whatever that was) for the sheer pleasure of wandering incognito through unfamiliar parts of town. Habitués of dubious little cafés knew him variously as a concert pianist, a retired colonial civil servant with some vague scandal in his past, an ex-lumberjack, a retired gambler, the son of an exiled Brazilian minister. He mixed with expatriate American actors dubbing films for a living, an IRA bomber on the run with a fund of amusing stories and a group of young men who, truthfully or not, claimed membership in the OAS. In short, he hadn't had as much fun since his acting days at university.

Inspector Claude Didier stuck his identity card under

the room clerk's cratered nose and snapped it shut, causing a miniature updraft that caught a strand of his straggly forelock and wafted it gently upwards. 'Service de Documentation Intérieur,' said Baudoin. 'The old woman, Thursday night, white hair, black overcoat. Whom did she visit and for how long?'

The clerk returned his stare dully and ran a finger around the inside of his collar. *'Bordel de Dieu.* Here they come again. The boss is pissed off about the laundry service, those pricks from the vice squad have been in again, and now this *salaud* from some cop shop he'd never even heard of.' He thought suddenly of his cottage in the Dordogne and the name over the door copied from a villa further down the valley. 'Mon Repos' – chic that; painted it himself.

'I'm waiting.'

'I don't remember. It might have been . . . '

'Listen, my little friend, how many little old ladies do you get in here. If we have to go through all the rooms to refresh your memory, who knows who or what we may find there . . . some of the girls from the café across the street, do you think?'

'Number twelve.'

Baudoin turned the register around and found the name: Louis Delpire, Montreal. He glanced at the board and saw that the key for number twelve was hanging on the hook.

'Let's go,' he said.

The lift stopped with a jolt on the first floor and the clerk went first down the hall. A black with ritual facial scars stepped into the passage, hesitated for a split second with his hand on the knob and then slid past them towards the lift, keeping as close to the wall as possible.

Half-hearted daylight barely made it through the room's grimy window panes. Baudoin switched on the light. Outside it was raining again. In the distance a bright red first-class metro carriage sandwiched between grey ones flickered briefly behind the crisscross girders of an overhead crossing and disappeared behind a building. The wallpaper had never been designed with that shade of carpet in mind. On the bedside table a cheap lamp with a hideous flounced shade glowed raspberry. The woodwork had been painted so many times that all of the original detail was obliterated. It could have used another coat. The usual props of a transient womanless hotel room.

The night-table drawer held a half-used box of matches from a Montreal nightclub. A cheap deal chest of drawers contained nothing unexpected: some shirts back from the laundry still pinned in grey paper, underwear, socks.

'How old?' said Baudoin, shutting the bottom drawer. There were no paperbacks or magazines . . . shaving articles on the wash-stand, wads of grey, smudged cleansing tissue in the waste basket. A painted metal ashtray advertised Cinzano.

'Who?'

'The man, of course, *mon cher*, the man who rents this room.'

'Middle aged – about fifty I guess.'

'You guess. How tall?'

'Taller than me. About your height.'

'Hair?'

'Grey, like yours – only darker.'

'Eyes?'

'I don't know . . . blue maybe.'

'Anything else?'

'*Comment?*'

'Scars, limp, nervous tic, one arm, drinks all night. Come, come, *mon brave*, use your imagination.' Baudoin was surprised to find that his annoyance was not feigned. He could have swatted the little bugger just to see him wince.

'He wears a sort of silver bracelet and talks with a funny accent.'

'French Canadian,' thought Baudoin, moving to the wardrobe. The suit pockets were empty. Labels told him nothing except that they came from Antoine's, Montreal. Impossible to deduce anything about their owner. That kind of ready-to-wear was all alike. A rather expensive empty leather bag on the floor bore an Air France tag and a sticker from the Hotel El Presidente – Acapulco. Baudoin glanced at his watch, took one last look around and switched off the light. A blank. An absolute blank. Who or what was this Louis Delpire from Montreal? What was his business with Madame Vallette?

They took the stairs and the clerk scuttled across the lobby to the desk.

'How long did the old woman stay?' asked Baudoin.

'I don't know. I go off at ten.'

'What was he wearing when he went out?'

'A raincoat . . . dark . . . black, I think . . . and one of those cloth rain hats.'

'Name . . .' said Baudoin, opening his notebook.

'But you already have it . . .' the clerk glanced down at the registry. 'Louis . . .'

'Your name, *mon chou*.'

'Bézier, Robert Bézier.'

'Ciao, Robert, I may send you a postcard. A thousand thanks for your valuable time. And . . .

don't mention my little visit to our Canadian friend, will you.' Baudoin smiled from the doorway and stepped into the street.

'Bastard,' said the room clerk.

14

The rain started to come down again in perfectly vertical streaks against the leaden sky, like scratches on an old silent movie print, transforming wet, black asphalt into a field of dancing white dandelions that stretched away to where the hotel's reflected red neon glimmered in the gutter. A sleek Citroën sped by like a hungry shark trailing a plume of spray. A perfect day for hovering in doorways. No one had gone in or come out of the hotel all afternoon, except one of the girls from the misnamed Soleil du Midi down the street and one of her clients. They stayed for perhaps twenty minutes and parted forever in the doorway . . . no Canadians in black raincoats, no fragile old ladies on incomprehensible errands. Nothing. Baudoin turned up his collar, pulled down his dripping hat brim and followed the girl into the café.

Choosing a table near the door where he could keep the hotel entrance in view, he sat down and looked about him: a number of rather fleshy and flashy ladies, well equipped for the weather with colourful umbrellas and smart rainwear in bright plastic, occupied tables and some of the booths along one wall. Quite a lot of mutual grooming and good-natured banter was going on: a flaming redhead with a towering pompadour, winning a point at *bulotte*, slapped a card noisily on the table; a petite blonde with aerodynamic buttocks tightly encased in black leather surrendered with closed eyes to the pleasures of an energetic back scratch administered by a hefty colleague with shoulder-length platinum hair. Except for the super-chic rainwear, oversized handbags and heavy make-up, they might have been a group of girls on a school-holiday outing trapped by the weather in some Alpine refuge. Reclining majestically at their feet on the grimy mosaic, the proprietor's gigantic Alsatian, feigning sleep, suffered his head to be scratched. One ear, like a defective compass needle, oscillated between WSW and SSE – the other permanently indicated the pole. A sprinkling of male customers ignored – and were ignored by – the ladies: a plump *garagiste*, deep in conversation with the *patron*, wearing a once-blue beret and overalls so impregnated with grease as to resemble old leather, balanced his enormous behind on a slender bar stool. The walls had once been decorated with Toulouse-Lautrec reproductions whose lighter tones had through the years merged with the basic wall colour, roughly that of wet cigarette butts. La Goulue in mid-cancan showed her frilly pantaloons to top-hatted *boulevardiers* at the Moulin Rouge. The gloom outside the steamy windows past which swam indistinct figures like deep sea fish behind the portholes of a bathysphere, creating an enclosed, almost subaqueous atmosphere, the lurid fluorescent lighting reflected from the bottles behind the bar and from the patent-leather shoes and dark glasses of a snappily dressed and sinister black man cleaning his nails at a corner table, all this produced a whisper of depravity that Baudoin, behind his moustache, was finding positively exhilarating.

The platinum blonde stuck out her tongue at him

and, cupping a breast, jerked her head towards the door. Baudoin retrieved his cigarettes from the swipe of a greasy rag, wielded by a muscular waiter with bilious green, cerulean and violet tattoos evoking disreputable little waterfront cafés, who relayed his order to the *patron*.

'How's business, Lucette?' the *garagiste* called out to one of the girls.

'Go screw yourself, René,' she called back good-naturedly. René mumbled something to the proprietor and they both laughed loudly. Baudoin looked around involuntarily at the mention of his name and met the girl's frankly appraising gaze: he had been the object of her professional curiosity for some minutes. Moving over to his table, she treated him to a girlish smile in which all of her features participated.

'*Vous permettez, Monsieur?*' she said, sitting down. 'What delightful weather!' Depths of décolleté were gift-wrapped in a transparent plastic raincoat. Vaguely she reminded him of Gaby except for a more generously proportioned figure. Her blonde hair was tied back with a blue hair ribbon.

'I believe this is where I offer you a drink, Mademoiselle,' said Baudoin.

'Why not?' she said and decided to have a real one instead of the fizzy soft stuff she normally drank during working hours; the rain had killed business for the rest of the evening anyway. 'I don't suppose, Theo,' she called out to the waiter, 'we could get something to drink? *Etwas zu trinken*, you lousy *Boche!*' Baudoin ordered a Pernod and another whiskey and glanced past her through the window. Stood up by a girl, thought Lucette, wondering all the time what he would be like without the wig. Or following somebody. Something about the moustache brought to mind an actor still in his make-up, or an embezzler bound for Brazil. She thought suddenly of Marcel, but no fugitive in his right mind would come into a café so much under the eye of the police. Not a cop either; cops don't run around in disguises. A kink maybe – likes wigs instead of high heels. She sighed.

Baudoin caught out of the corner of his eye a black blur at the window and looked straight into the face of a priest in a black hat who stared intently through the misted pane for a moment, before the image dissolved and swam away.

'The *curé*,' said Lucette, '... looking for me.' She made a careful arrangement of Baudoin's cigarettes and matchbox. 'One of my regular clients,' she said and looked up suddenly from under black lashes to see whether her words had shocked. 'He won't come in here, we meet by appointment.' Baudoin shook the empty matchbox and she lit his cigarette with a heavy gold lighter. 'A present,' she said, 'from a man whose name you would recognise. He pays me to impersonate a corpse – white gown, flowers, candles at my head and feet, spooky music . . .'

'That's all?' asked Baudoin. 'There must be more.'

'There's more,' said Lucette, giggling, 'because I can hear funny noises in the dark but he gets furious if I try to peek.'

'A necrophile without the courage of his convictions, one would say,' said Baudoin, emptying his glass and nodding at Theo. He could sense the curiosity behind Lucette's anecdotes and was beginning to like her as much for her somewhat hardbitten sense of humour as for her more obvious attractions. He found himself entertaining an unseemly intention.

'Then there is the gentleman who combines a fondness for chocolate . . . ' She paused for a moment in her account as Theo, scowling at Baudoin, set down the drinks between them with more noise than was absolutely necessary. 'Don't mind him,' said Lucette. 'He thinks I should take up nursing or secretarial work.' Baudoin was wondering, in fact, how a personable, intelligent girl like Lucette had gone on the game. 'By the incremental crossing of conventional barriers,' he thought, answering his own question. 'One day you buy a wig and a few months later you're impersonating policemen and consorting with prostitutes.'

'Listen Lucette,' he said, 'it's a nasty night and my apartment is warm. If you are not engaged for the evening, I prefer *chez moi* to the charming little hotel that you probably know of' – and reading her thoughts, 'I hate chocolate . . . as for my other tastes, they are utterly, boringly traditional; no need to bring a trunkful of equipment.'

'You understand' she said, 'that my fee would be proportionately larger.'

'But certainly, Lucette. Should we go?'

Huddled together under Lucette's umbrella, they unsteadily crossed the glistening pavement toward a taxi miraculously appearing in the driving rain – Baudoin maintaining an overstudied imitation of sobriety in spite of legs that seemed suddenly a centimetre longer than usual and struck the ground a split second too early. Their uncoordinated leap over a rivulet running in the gutter seemed somehow hilarious. Handing Lucette into the back with elaborate old-world gallantry and casting a last glance at the hotel entrance over the taxi's rain-beaded top, Baudoin settled in beside her. It was now late at night.

They were approaching the Place St Germain when Baudoin took off his hat, his hair and his moustache and put them in his pocket. Lucette giggled, prepared for the head to follow, or an arm, and tweaked his nose to see if it was real – moving Baudoin to enfold her small hand in a clumsy paw; he attempted to mutter something in her ear but his upper lip, without the moustache, seemed to her inordinately long and she went off into a delightful peal of laughter which brought the driver's head around; the expression on his face as he gave change to an entirely different gentleman provoked another outburst. He looked after them thoughtfully as Lucette, still laughing, weaving slightly on her extravagantly high heels, attempted to ape Baudoin's exaggerated tiptoe across the marble floor of the *entrée* – mysteriously two centimetres lower than he remembered it. There was some fumbling with keys and articles of clothing in the lift.

Once inside the apartment, he tugged experimentally at the blue ribbon and her hair uncoiled, waiting for a shake of her head to free it. '*Un instant, chéri,*' she murmured and with unerring instinct headed down the hallway toward the bathroom. Baudoin went to the kitchen in search of a suddenly remembered bottle of champagne put away for another, superficially similar, occasion. Pushing aside leftover parts of his gas heater that had defied reassembly, he fumbled through several drawers and searched everywhere on the shelves before remembering that a corkscrew is not necessary to open champagne; and having established that anchor of sober rationality in an incoherent universe, decided to get to the bottom of the problem posed by the variable length of his legs.

Giggles from the bedroom. Lucette, at that moment wearing little else besides Professor Cendrar's grey whiskers (attached with some sticky stuff found in the bathroom), was displaying her full body to the shocked gaze of Aunt Berthe's wardrobe mirror. The giggles grew louder as with sudden ribald inspiration she added another bushy brown beaver – attaching the points that go over the ears just below her prominent pelvic bones – where it modestly covered a smaller, blondish one. A beribboned pince-nez and a black homburg completed the effect.

Baudoin, sans trousers (which he had draped neatly over the chair arm), manipulating a tape measure with that singleminded deliberation of the very drunk, in an effort to establish certain fundamental truths, was measuring the length of his legs. His research was interrupted by a vision no less unsettling to logic and order, as Lucette pirouetting into the room struck a ballet pose just inside the door and flourished one hand aloft. Baudoin regarded the naked, bearded lady wearing an obscenely gargantuan, bushy brown sporran with the same deliberation carried over from his other investigations before collapsing onto the settee in a fit of helpless laughter – temporarily robbed of the capacity most appropriate to the occasion. 'And now, *mon grand*,' said Lucette, tripping across the room to his rescue.

Politely ignoring the short-coming most dreaded by gentlemen (which incidentally invalidated the endearment), Lucette helped him off with his jacket (automatically noting the disposition of the wallet which it contained) and removing his shirt and tie, began to apply certain amazingly simple but effective measures

– combined with a quick technical examination, for Lucette was nothing if not professional – that restored to him the requisite capability. The settee creaked as she moved expertly to accommodate his bulk, went on creaking; the pince-nez fell down a crack between the upholstery and someone's knee; Baudoin's wiry, brown chest hair mingled with Professor Cendrar's grey academic ones; Aunt Berthe's portrait should have been turned to the wall . . . those who have ever made love to a bearded lady will recognise that special thrill. In short, or rather at length, Baudoin then and there was able to disprove, at least for that once, traditional wisdom concerning the effect of alcohol on masculine vigour. He had on other occasions, in fact, observed the opposite phenomenon.

Lucette, working overtime in various attitudes and bizarre locations, was to learn this at repeated intervals throughout the course of the evening: sliding down the lino towards the kitchen where she had been overtaken on some forgotten errand; half in and half out of the wardrobe, surprised while choosing the proper necktie to complement the moustache she now wore under one ear, and through a mouthful of which Baudoin was mumbling some other girl's name, as, stifling a yawn, she watched their mutual exertions in the mirror and with that ambidexterous, polyrhythmic facility known to concert pianists, jazz drummers and accomplished whores – combining a left-hand pianissimo played on the lumbar nodes with a certain right-handed, nether accompaniment – endeavoured to orchestrate his *lentissima con dilgencia* toward a crashing crescendo (moaning brass, sobbing violins).

Baudoin awoke late the next morning in his own

bed and stared at the ceiling; it was important to remember how he came to be there. A continuing, intermittent buzz filled his ears but he could not decide whether it originated inside his head or somewhere in the room. Devastatingly cheerful, late morning sun poured across the bed. Ludmilla sat on his feet with one leg extended like a ballet dancer at the exercise bar noisily worrying a tangled place on her abdomen. She lost interest suddenly, still maintaining the pose – as if the music had suddenly stopped – and gazed vacantly towards the half-open window where a blundering bee bumped repeatedly, idiotically against the panes. Wondering how such a thick-headed species could have survived through the eons, Baudoin pushed Ludmilla aside and crawled out of bed prepared to execute it for stupidity when suddenly, to its own astonishment (lucky ricochet), it shot out into space and dissolved in the green square of the window. Baudoin switched off the still burning bedside lamp, took three aspirin (avoiding his reflection in the medicine cabinet mirror), and stepping over a trodden pair of dark glasses somewhat resembling a mashed beetle, a badly dented bowler hat, and other oddments of costume littering the floor, went barefoot into the sitting-room stepping as carefully as on floating logs. His wallet and a note from Lucette lay on the desk; only half the money was gone. Good, brave, honest Lucette! He smiled, remembering some fragment of the night before and, wincing at another recollection, opened the window: A calm, sunny, Monday morning. On the bench near the bus stop, Madam Q. fed a coterie of field-grey clockwork pigeons who strutted about militaristically, heads bobbing, stepping on their own shadows. The white-jacketed waiter from the Reine Blanche, balancing a loaded tray, made his usual midday trip down the pavement to number 163. Two Carmelite nuns went by under full sail and then the baker's boy on a bicycle with a bundle of *baguettes*. A gaunt *afficheur* unslung his ladder and began to paste the face of a blue-eyed blonde purveying DOP Shampoo who was then covered over with a poster advertising '*Zazi Dans le Métro*'. A house painter on the fifth floor stopped work, wiped his neck with a red bandanna and looked down into the street. The windows opposite were as non-committal as ever. His next visit, Baudoin realised, was going to be much riskier: there was no longer any way he could predict the old woman's movements. He stood there for a moment longer and then began to go through his desk looking for Concepta's key-ring.

15

A door opened somewhere overhead and Baudoin, in a panic, opened the inner swing-doors, stopping the lift a half-meter short of its proper alignment on the second floor. Making a great deal of noise, he scrambled over the sill into the darkened landing and began to go through his pockets as if looking for those elusive keys. The lift hummed, started upward and after a pause punctuated by the clank of the door closing overhead, ho-hummed and started down again. Its interior light sought the wall, slid downward and spread across the carpet. Baudoin ventured a glance over his shoulder and saw tan trousers and a dark raincoat descending then, shaded by his hat brim, the face of a darkly complexioned or suntanned man. A silver identity bracelet shone dully as he adjusted his collar and sank out of sight, leaving the landing once again in darkness.

Baudoin hesitated and then started down the stairs. He couldn't be sure which of the two doors on the landing above had opened and closed. The man fitted the room clerk's description but so did several thousand other men in the city. He gained the *entrée* out of breath and opened the door to the street. No one. The man was nowhere in sight.

Monday, later in the week, he got his chance – but as it happened, he almost missed it. The weather had been hot and muggy for several days. In the street below, intermittently audible above the sound of occasional passing cars, the desultory movement of a half-hearted night breeze, stirring into movement the plane trees that partially obscured the entrance to number 180, simulated tantalisingly the sound of falling rain. Baudoin, in his undershirt, returning with a cold bottle of beer from the kitchen and pushing Ludmilla off the armchair by the windows, noticed that during his brief absence a taxi had pulled up before the building across the street. Remaining crouched in his half-sitting position and craning further forward to penetrate the screen of foliage, he just got a glimpse of the old lady crossing the pavement and then a moment's clear view as she bent to instruct the driver and got into the back seat. Baudoin was already in the bedroom pulling on a shirt as the taxi moved away from the curb.

Her elderly neighbour, a bookseller who lived on the second floor left, was just stepping into the street as, minutes later, Baudoin approached the entrance. He walked straight on past and stopped before the illuminated window of a dental supply house, fingering the warm keys in his pocket and pretending to study a gruesome pair of extractors gleaming in a showcase. A headline skittered down the street and attached itself to his trouser leg for a moment then sailed on toward the corner. He cast a glance over his shoulder at the man's receding figure, hesitated a moment longer and buzzed open the door. The concierge had long since gone to bed; Baudoin went quickly past her window in semi-darkness to the lift.

Selecting the proper key from Concepta's ring, he unlocked the door, closed it behind him and stood for a moment in the darkness, listening to the ticking of the clock. Through the open double doors leading to the *salon* on his right, an open window framed a rectangle of dull orange night sky; he moved in that direction thumbing the switch of his flashlight. The damn thing didn't work. His knee banged against something in the dark and he fell heavily, swearing. The flashlight came on as it hit the floor, spilling its beam as it rolled, and came to rest near the window, lighting up a wedge of bare floorboards and a semi-circular patch of wall. Baudoin retrieved it on all fours, closed the window and, pulling the drapes, shone the flashlight about the room. Its beam traversed a rolled up section of carpet, then a pile of loose parquet floorboards, transfixed briefly the cat peering from under the table whose eyes blazed spectrally, and found the light switch. Baudoin turned on the lights and looked about him trying to come to terms with the chaos that met his eye.

A gang of exterminators probing for dry rot, working in close collaboration with a demented decorator, had apparently been set loose on the room: A stack of tiles prised loose from the disused fireplace, whose raised metal closure obscenely revealed its soot-blackened interior, shared a corner with volumes from the empty glass-fronted bookcase and a heavily framed landscape; wallpaper dangled grotesquely where the Bokhara once hung; a length of skirting board leaned insolently against the wall. Nothing was where he remembered it, nothing in its proper place. Sheet-shrouded armchairs huddled together, whispering, in the middle of the floor like a conclave of squat, bulgy ghosts, others against the wall, aghast. The writing desk now stood in the dining room; the dining-room table, loaded with bric-à-brac, had crept part way into the *salon*. Only the family photographs on the mantel retained their original positions. The commander gazed back at Baudoin with annoying unconcern.

His bewilderment slowly giving way to something very akin to outrage, Baudoin squeezed past an armchair holding the African idol in its lap and, frowning at a pair of decorator's white overalls left lying on the floor, went through to the stairs. Stepping over a missing tread, he turned left at the top, puffing slightly and perspiring, went down the hallway to the bedroom and switched on the light: a dressing table, built-in bookcase, double bed with a flounced satin coverlet upon which an old-fashioned child's doll with closed china lids lay dreaming, garish dressing-gown lying across the bolster, and in the corner a smart new travelling case. His bearded reflection turned to face him as he opened the wardrobe door and, smiling slightly, mimicked his movements as he fingered the garments, smelling faintly of lavender, hanging there on crocheted hangers, then diminished to a silver sliver and slipped inside again as he turned to the luggage. It contained a woman's pastel-blue, lightweight top coat, some print dresses and skirts, blouses, shoes, and a collection of female underwear . . . 'Fifty years of severe black and now a new wardrobe?' he thought . . . 'For the visit to Carcassonne perhaps?' But then he remembered that the trip to Carcassonne was his own invention. The 'dressing-gown' turned out to be a pair of men's red striped pajamas! . . . Clearly there was more to the widow Vallette than met the eye! 'Preposterous!' he said out loud, thinking the unthinkable: ' . . . A seventy-year-old woman with a boyfriend? . . . Absurd! . . . and yet . . . midnight rendezvous with creepy Canadians in disreputable hotels . . . redecorating the nest, new clothes, new luggage . . . for what? . . . an elopement to Canada? Ridiculous!'

He was now sitting on the arm of a chair before the dressing table with the pajama bottoms still in his hand. His beard itched ferociously and he stuffed it in his pocket – accidentally brushing from the surface of the table a wad of cleansing tissue like one he remembered from somewhere. He picked it up and held it to his nostrils . . . cold cream, the sweetish odour of cold cream . . . cold cream and something else vaguely familiar . . . And then he remembered.

Simultaneously with the recognition came a burst of recollection: He saw himself again, perspiring in his make-up under the lights, unable to scratch his maddeningly itching nose – the tan ring of make-up staining the shirt cuff of the arm that held up an inverted prop sword as a crucifix to ward off his father's ghost: Baudoin, the melancholy Dane, in a school production of *Hamlet*, terrified of that multiple beast lurking in the darkness behind the footlights – and of going blank again on that line where he always went blank:

'Angels and ministers of Grace defend us!' he cried out loud in English – and after twenty years went blank again. He stared amazed at the crumpled tissue in his hand and began to rummage rapidly through the dressing-table drawers: found the familiar, fat, paper-wrapped sticks of greasy make-up in a leatherette case, together with some brushes of various sizes, powder, powder puff, and a fat jar of cold cream.

'Oh answer me!' he declaimed, slamming the drawer and walking quickly down the hall to the bathroom, 'Let me not burst in ignorance!' Flinging open the door, 'Say why is this? wherefore?'

A man's razor and a tube of shaving cream lay on the basin; from a hook hung two terrycloth robes. Inside the medicine cabinet among the familiar small, squarish brown ones was a large bottle of hydrogen peroxide and another containing a commercial blue hair rinse. 'A little old, white-haired lady, who goes religiously to the hairdresser, with a cabinet full of hair bleach' he thought, replacing the bottles and shutting the cabinet door. 'Seems, madame!' he muttered, switching off the light and starting toward the stairs, 'Nay, it is . . . 'tis not alone my inky cloak, good mother, nor customary suits of solemn black . . . ' Descending the stairs, 'These indeed seem, for they are actions that a man . . . (or a woman) might play.'

He sat down in an armchair, sniffed the tissue again, and deep in thought, looked around the room. The African fertility goddess glowered from the shadows; the clock whizzed, clunked twice and got ready to strike the hour. Baudoin stood up suddenly and went into the kitchen where he found the cognac bottle and pouring a quantity into a glass swallowed a mouthful. He carried the glass into the *salon*, sat down again, took another sip, lit a cigarette, discarding the match in a handy Chinese bowl, stood up and started toward the writing desk near the window. Halfway there the photographs on the mantel caught his eye: the commander, the graduating class, and Madame Vallette herself in what he had supposed was her wedding dress, smiling radiantly at the camera. Something about that photograph bothered him. For one thing, wedding photographs of that day were always deadpan, serious – and here she was smiling like a movie star at a première . . . and where was the groom? Wedding photos usually include the groom. He picked it up to examine it more closely and then he noticed something else: the photograph had been made with a flash!

. . . A movie star? . . . or an actress in a costume?

With a knife from the kitchen he slit the paper binding sealing the velveteen backing and slipping the print out from behind the glass, turned it over. A carelessly rubber-stamped legend on the back began: 'Edward Mortenson, Theatrical Composites' in smeary purple, almost black letters, followed by ' . . . and Production Stills' (royal to medium) then 'Montreal 77' – something, something, in light, fading-to-lighter lavender – the last two digits of the telephone number fading out entirely before Baudoin had time to read them. He stood staring at it, completely oblivious of the cat, which, with back arched and quivering tail, was rubbing ecstatically against his legs.

Slipping the photograph back inside the frame and replacing it with the others, he swallowed more cognac and carried his glass to the desk. Under the telephone was a sheet of paper covered with the old woman's doodled signature repeated across the entire page. Stooping, he retrieved from the waste-paper basket two more similar sheets and a dusty, crumpled ball of notepaper which he smoothed out on the blotter. Scrawled across it were the abbreviated words: '40^e D^{on} 2^e Section' – words he'd seen before somewhere during his previous reconnaissance. Some quick rummaging through the drawers and cubby holes produced what he was looking for in a brown paper folder under the blue one containing the widow's copy of their agreement. Clipped together with some household bills was an estimate, now accompanied by a receipted bill, from a certain Duclos et Fils for repairs to the family mausoleum – 'Cimetière de l'Est, fortieth division, second section.' Baudoin sat down at the desk and compared the estimate with the scrap of paper, remained sitting lost in thought for several minutes. The clock cleared its throat and struck the half hour; his cigarette almost burned his fingers and he doused it in the cognac. Baudoin looked at his watch, copied the four words into his notebook using a silver pencil left lying on the desk, very like one he'd lost somewhere, crumpled up and discarded the scrap of notepaper and standing up, walked slowly towards the door. He paused, still meditating, with his hand on the knob and then remembering to replace the cognac bottle, rinse his glass and, yes, retrieve the burnt match from the Chinese bowl, turned out all the lights, pulled back the drapes and opened the window: a light rain was falling after all. He went out and closed the door behind him.

16

The cemetery known popularly as Père Lachaise, officially designated Le Cimetière de l'Est, lies at the end of the Avenue de la République in the nineteenth Arrondissement near the Métro stop that bears its name. Probably the most famous in the world – not counting that one in California – it is, in the words of the old cliché that kept running through Baudoin's mind as he trudged up its main avenue, a veritable city of the dead.

A lot of construction and demolition was certainly going on: mounds of raw earth thrown up by snorting, bright yellow tractors; marble slabs lying about like extracted dinosaurs' teeth. 'Enough noise to raise the dead,' Baudoin thought, not in the least bit amused. Consulting the map handed him by a guardian at the main gate, he set off down a winding, tree-lined avenue past row upon row of mausoleums in a hundred different styles. Jumbled together as in some neurasthenic *beaux arts* nightmare, bedecked and bestrewn with an excrescence of real and stylised plant life permanently petrified in marble and bronze or embalmed in plastic wrappings – like the bouquet, bought from the florist near the Métro station that he carried under one arm – they achieved the very summit of bourgeois ostentation.

Astounding juxtapositions assailed the eye: Gothic

cast-iron tendrils and squiggles cheek by jowl with *art nouveau* bronze fronds and furbelows, cupolas, trefoils, bulbous rotundas, baroque gazebos, rococo extravaganzas; severe modern monoliths of shiny, black marble were incongruously interposed between scaled-down granite bank vaults and dwarf stock exchanges in what could be called the financial funerary style; some tilted at crazy angles as if the market had just taken a sudden plunge. (Many were closed, presumably locked, he observed, but an equal number stood wide open, as if the occupant had just stepped out for a stroll in the fine weather.)

Supreme over all was an impression of dilapidation and decay: marble veneer peeled like wet cardboard, pilasters bulged obscenely, roofs collapsed in slow motion. Not a few of the most decrepit, tenants long since evicted, were marked for demolition with painted red X's. Some of these, he noted, were being used as repositories for workmen's tools and paraphernalia – including the inevitable half-empty bottle of red wine.

He lost his way temporarily in a section with more than the usual number of bad bronze sculptures – numerous Niobes, all tears, falling about in stylised attitudes of inconsolable grief – and stopped to consult the map. A very important person with ferocious verdigris whiskers eyed him suspiciously from atop a plinth as Baudoin re-oriented himself and set off to his left. He didn't have far to go: the flagstones gave way to a gravel path climbing to the left and suddenly there it was: 'La Famille Vallette', carved and gilded above the door and lower down the supernaturally illogical but somehow touching inscription: *'concession en perpétuité*, allotment in perpetuity No. 116'.

The iron door with its plaited, wrought-iron grill was newly painted and to his intense relief stood slightly ajar. There was no one about and he pushed it open, expecting it to squeak, but it moved back easily, revealing a small altar shelf with a withered bouquet in an inexpensive vase below the inscription: 'Commander Eugene Vallette, 1885–1944'. Incised below that was a row of enamel and gilt military decorations which Baudoin could not identify. Marble slabs inset with bronze lifting sockets formed the floor. He bent down to examine a new scratch where an implement of some kind had apparently slipped, leaving a raw scar on the marble; the adjoining slab had been chipped at the edge as if by insertion of a crowbar. The joints were clean and free of dust. There was no doubt that the vault had been recently opened.

Baudoin removed the wilted roses and placed his own bouquet in the vase, closed the door and started back down the path. He discarded the roses in a wooden bin and turned to look back, wondering whether it was by presentiment or coincidence that she had undertaken such timely repairs. He was also wondering how they had managed to get her over the wall and how he was going to persuade the police to have a look in that vault without answering a lot of embarrassing questions.

17

The problem of embarrassing questions still preoccupied Baudoin later that same day as he followed a uniformed sergeant of police down a long dingy corridor to an even dingier third-floor office. The man behind the desk did not look up or acknowledge Baudoin's presence, merely nodding his head once or twice in response to whatever information the sergeant was addressing to the top of his nearly bald head as he went on shuffling through a stack of dog-eared reports in coloured cardboard folders spread out on the scrofulous blotter. He did not in the least resemble Baudoin's conception of a policeman: dark well-cut suit, tasteful tie; his few remaining strands of hair a bit too slicked down over the cranium perhaps, but Baudoin knew without seeing them that his shoes were not thick-soled. The only thing policeman-like about Inspector Claude Bernard was the half-smoked cigar lying in an ashtray which he now retrieved and the neutral stare which he fixed on Baudoin as he motioned him to a seat near his desk. Their interview got off on the wrong foot right from the start.

'You wish to report a death, Monsieur.' It was a statement, not a question.

'That is correct.'

'And the name of the deceased?'

'Madame Honorine Vallette.'

'At what address?'
'180 Boulevard St Germain, but she's not there now.'
'I see. Where exactly is the deceased?'
'In a mausoleum.'
'I see.' Bernard shot a cold glance at the sergeant and put down his pen. 'Which particular mausoleum would that be?'
'The family Vallette mausoleum, Père Lachaise, fortieth division, second section.'
'You must excuse me, Monsieur . . .'
'Baudoin.'
'. . . Thank you, you must excuse me, Monsieur Baudoin. I'm a bit confused. You say that a certain Honorine Vallette, deceased, is at present in her own family vault in a cemetery.'
'That is correct.'
'May I ask, Monsieur Baudoin, why you consider this a police matter? The family mausoleum would appear to be a perfectly normal place for a deceased person.'
'I'm not making myself clear, I'm afraid. You see, her daughter put her there.'
'Her daughter put her there.'
'That is correct.'
Bernard passed a hand over the top of his head. 'Perhaps I'm a bit dense today, Monsieur Baudoin, but I am having some difficulty in understanding why you consider it police business if a daughter buries her mother in the family mausoleum.'
'That's just it, you see. She wasn't buried.'
Bernard stubbed out his cigar and leaned forward. He looked at the sergeant and then back at Baudoin. 'Forgive me, Monsieur Baudoin, but we seem to get

no further. The deceased is *in* the family vault but was not *buried* in the family vault. If she was not buried in the family vault how did she come to *be* in the family vault?'

'I mean there was no funeral. She's not supposed to be dead.'

Baudoin's later recollection of the rest of that day and the three days that followed was a confused jumble of disconnected vignettes: long intervals during which nothing at all seemed to be happening interspersed with moments of frantic activity when everything seemed to be happening at once. The red tape required for authorisation to open a grave is a lengthy process even for the police – especially if the necessary official to sign the necessary paper cannot be found, having decided to take a long lunch hour, it being a Friday and the weekend coming up, and so forth and so on . . . so that it was not till five o'clock that they started on the interminable drive to Père Lachaise in a black Citroën, during which Baudoin responded with a makeshift rigmarole, leaving out more than it included, to Bernard's questions about how he, Baudoin, had discovered whatever it was he thought he'd discovered – a balancing act which did not satisfy Bernard, who kept squinting sideways at Baudoin while boring thoughtfully in his ear with a little finger.

And it was not till six-thirty that Baudoin found himself for the second time that day standing a little way off down the path from the Family Vallette mausoleum with Inspector Bernard and the head guardian while a workman in blue overalls assisted a uniformed policeman (also in blue) to grapple up one of the marble slabs that formed the floor and wrestle it out through the narrow doorway – or was it the other way around, for they were certainly getting in each other's way a good deal – the policeman's képi getting knocked off in the process and rolling a little way down the path to stop at Bernard's feet; Bernard picking it up absently and holding it in his hand while a flashlight was sent for on the run from the guardian's hut because nobody had thought to bring one and nothing was discernible in the blackness under the floor and nobody, even the police, who were supposed to be inured to such things, was especially eager to climb down there and feel around in the dark – although they all tried to crowd through the door at the same time trying to see something; and finally a flashlight being handed to the policemen by a subguardian all out of breath; the workman standing back deferentially dusting off the knees of his blue overalls; Bernard still holding the hat because there didn't seem to be anything else to do with it – its owner, face covered with a handkerchief, occupied just then shining the flashlight down into the blackness for what seemed an interminable moment and then looking back over his shoulder at Bernard, still holding the hat, and nodding.

After that of course there was nothing to do but wait: wait and pace up and down the sitting room chain-smoking, asking himself a thousand questions; drawn to the front windows every fifteen minutes to stare across the street at her apartment (*his* apartment he suddenly realised and wondered why the fact seemed so flat and uninteresting) – although there was absolutely nothing to see after that first morning when the black Citroën pulled up and Bernard went into the building accompanied by a uniformed policeman – only to re-emerge a few hours later with the daughter, dressed in her own pastel-blue coat this time, but still wearing her mother's hair, accompanied by a dark man with a black raincoat over his arm, that Baudoin only glimpsed as he got into the car. Her husband? . . . Lover? . . . who was he really, this . . . this Canadian and how did he think he, they, could get away with it, and what exactly were they trying to get away with anyway? How had they managed it, trundling bodies around in the dead of night right under his nose – for it must have happened right under his nose. How ironic to peer out of the window for months on end at *femmes de ménage*, delivery boys, moving shadows on the curtains and miss the one dramatic moment. How stupid to have catalogued her shopping trips and missed her murder – asleep in his armchair probably, with the whole macabre escapade taking place a literal stone's throw away. What could have justified such a monstrous charade? Why tear up her apartment – his apartment? What were they looking for anyway?

18

What a dismal, incongruous rigmarole for such a summer's day. Any competent director would have staged it on a bleak November morning: bare black branches against a winter sky, a dull brown, disconsolate sparrow or two etcetera. Even the sound effects were inept: somewhere overhead, in the high, murmuring plane trees, an irrelevant blackbird commented inanely at all the wrong moments. Over the path and Bernard's polished, pink dome played shifting leaf patterns – now fading out abruptly as a cloud's shadow moved hastily up the path to soften for a moment the new varnished rawness of the cheap wooden coffin with its glittering brass handles resting on rough carpenter's trestles before the mausoleum. Some neighbouring poplars held still for a moment as if listening to something very far away and then commenced to whisper among themselves – masking the monotonous drone of a bored, black-frocked priest, interminably intoning his mumbo jumbo who, at the crucial moment, managed to forget entirely the deceased's name, covering his lapse with a cough and hastily deployed handkerchief and surreptitiously consulting a pencilled reminder in the flyleaf of his prayer book – enlivening thus the morning's tedium for a trio of comic-relief municipal sextons lounging there in the wings – bored and disgruntled because the mourners were few and the tip would be small – impatiently waiting for the priest to get it over with. Baudoin, somewhat jumpy, whom insomnia and all of those cigarettes had left with a strangely receptive void in his head, registering all these little details, which poised the entire charade on the very edge of slapstick, felt, as often happens, the first little stirring of incipient mirth; he looked down at his feet – where the flattened remains of Bernard's trampled cigar butt were still gamely sending up a wistfully comic little trail of smoke . . . no help; he tried staring straight ahead, but couldn't help fixing on the back of Bernard's pinkly glowing sunburned neck, hilarious in itself, where, perversely, at that precise moment, a busy, busy workaday wasp, infatuated by the brilliantine with which the last few remaining strands of Bernard's hair were plastered, steadfastly refusing Bernard's undignified wave-offs, was performing a frantic little aerobatic dance of pleasure and anticipation. Baudoin let slip a strangled guffaw; in another minute he was going to howl with insane laughter. Clenching his teeth tightly, he put a hand to his streaming eyes in a perfect though unconscious counterfeit of graveside grief and, shoulders still quivering, fixed his gaze beyond, where there appeared, shimmering and wavering through his tears, a frail, veiled figure all in black, holding herself very straight, eyes fixed straight ahead, flanked by a uniformed policeman: Madame Vallette herself, come to witness her own re-interment. No, that was hallucination; the illusion, however, persisted. Features obscured by a longer veil attached to the same or an exactly similar flat, black straw hat, the same severe black coat and silver hair, gloved hands clenched at her sides, stood the daughter. She hadn't even needed to buy mourning, thought Baudoin – the widow's weeds of her impersonation, serving now, ironically, their intended purpose.

A little way off, aloof, as if he had nothing to do with any of it, expressionless, eyes invisible behind yellow tinted sunglasses that somehow gave his suntanned features an unhealthy look, stood her husband. His silver identity bracelet glinted in the sun as he brushed back a lock of hair and Baudoin, completely sobered now, realised that he was looking at the man in the lift. What was his name? . . . Delpire or something . . . 'An unsavoury character,' Bernard had said . . . minor police record in Montreal . . . something about bad checks. Baudoin recalled those peculiar sheets of 'doodled' signatures on Madame Vallette's desk: of course, he'd been practising her signature. He tried again to read the daughter's expression behind her veil, imagining again the whole macabre business: the two of them waiting anxiously in the apartment for the cafés to close and the streets to empty, getting her body into that lift that haunted his dreams and down to the *entrée*, one of them propping her up while the other looks to see if the street is clear; an early morning drunk with a purple bruise on his forehead, haranguing an unseen audience, shambles in agonisingly slow motion down the street toward the Deux Magots (where the chairs had been stacked hours ago by hardworking Hautrive) and finally, finally, disappearing round the corner of the rue St Benoit. 'And then what?' he thought. 'Hail a passing cab?'

'A rented car probably,' Bernard supposed, or a van. And somehow Baudoin had missed it all – asleep in his chair, fifty metres across the street with the whole gruesome escapade taking place literally a stone's throw away. 'They just drove around,' Bernard had said, 'or parked in a quiet street, waiting for the cemetery to open, no need to heave her over the wall or anything so melodramatic. They could have wheeled her right through the main gate in broad daylight. little old heavily veiled widow in an invalid's folding wheel chair shaded by a parasol or an umbrella, supported by solicitous son-in-law in case she slumps a little, big bouquets blocking the view. No one would have noticed a thing. Happens every day in a cemetery. And if the daughter is distraught, maybe crying a little, why, what could be more natural? They're actors, don't forget – at least she is – and nothing would faze Delpire. The daughter wheels her around a little or simply parks at a nearby grave while he slips in and levers up one of the slabs. It's a tight squeeze with the door closed but it could be managed.' Anyway, they had managed it somehow, the whole distasteful business.

The priest finally droned to a halt; whereupon, with no lost motion, anticipating an early lunch break, the burial squad bundled the coffin into the vault as unceremoniously as a crate of old books being stored in the cellar (now you see me, now you don't), the senior of the three producing as if by magic a battered wooden box, once painted a bright spring green, containing sandy, ochre earth to be dispensed into the grave. Baudoin half-expected a brace of pigeons to fly out of his sleeve but instead, with the disdainful air of a city slicker performing card tricks for an avid group of local yokels, he produced from his hip pocket a small bright-metal scoop of the sort more appropriately used for dispensing bonbons from large glass jars into small sticky hands and offered it to Madame Vallette's daughter. Accepting it with a weary, meditative air, she sprinkled a token scoopful into the blackness at her feet and stuffing a folded bill into a specially partitioned compartment of the foreman's green box, turned away. Her husband declined with the sort of barely perceptible head shake directed at the auctioneer when the bidding has gone past one's limit and then Baudoin, not knowing how he came to be doing it because the foreman had mistaken him for a friend of the family (which in a queer sort of way . . .) or simply caught up in the ritual with no way to refuse without embarrassment – found himself dropping that yellowish earth – evoking sandcastles on a sunny southern beach – down into the darkness and remembering irrelevantly the vine-overgrown, covered well in the courtyard at Aunt Berthe's, down which as a boy in a far away summer he used to drop stones and hear, after a surprisingly long and delicious pause – while everything waited – the far away muffled splash. A lump rang hollowly on the coffin lid and for some reason which he could not have explained, Baudoin pushed an over-large tip into the corner of the box and stepped back.

And then they were going down the path towards the cobbled avenue and thence under a vaulted leafy canopy towards the police cars waiting at the gate; the slight squeak of Bernard's elegant shoes barely audible above the crunch of gravel under foot.

'He probably had it all worked out before his plane landed,' said Bernard after a while. 'No handwringing or hesitation for that gentleman.' Delpire and his wife were getting into another car. An officer shut the door and got into the front.

'It was his idea entirely,' said Bernard, settling back

against the seat and taking out his cigar case. The driver moved off smoothly and a heavily symbolic pram, pushed by an enormously pregnant young woman, slid backward past Baudoin's window. 'I suppose it would be easier to think of her as some sort of monster,' Bernard said, cracking the window to let out his cigar smoke. 'Actually, she wanted nothing to do with it – told me the whole story before I could get my notebook out. She came over for a brief visit – concerned, you know, not having seen her mother for a long time – and three days later the old lady died in her sleep. The full report isn't down yet but it was natural causes all right.' He leaned forward to roll the window all the way down; exhaust fumes mingled with cigar smoke. 'The rest was all his idea. . . . Ah, the mystery of the female heart – how do they get mixed up with these types? He must have flown over the same day and went straight to a hotel to stay out of sight. Something strange there, by the way. When we went round, the room clerk said we'd already been there two weeks ago.' He eyed Baudoin askance for the third time that day. Baudoin looked out the window at blurred vistas of the Avenue Ledru Rollin whizzing past; they stopped for a traffic light; a neighbouring car radio blared a popular tune. 'The heavier demolition would have been done in the daytime in case the neighbours noticed the noise,' Bernard went on. 'So he probably stayed overnight to avoid being seen going in and out. He had to avoid arousing the concierge's curiosity, you see. She thinks he may even have disguised himself . . . slightly far-fetched. She's not quite all there – drinks a bit. Of course, he may have posed as a workman to justify the noise.' (Again that glance . . . just a hint of a smile?)

'He's a very cool customer, is our Monsieur Delpire, I wouldn't put it past him. The cemetery idea was positively brilliant. *L'audace, mon ami, l'audace!* What better place for a body than in the family mausoleum? It's hardly even illegal!' Bernard smiled broadly and mopped his crown with a handkerchief. 'Of course, they would have had to act quickly in any case.'

'*Voilà*,' thought Baudoin, 'there he goes again.'

There were certain details connected with his little old lady's demise that he preferred not to think about. 'Post mortem morbidity' was one of them – 'on the dorsal aspect of the body' no less. Bernard positively dwelt on things like 'duration of rigor,' 'July heat'; he seemed to have a fascination for technical detail more appropriate in a medical examiner. Baudoin wondered whether he'd studied medicine – or was he merely getting a mischievous little kick out of Baudoin's squeamishness. 'Ice, lots of ice,' he kept saying, as if ordering a Ricard from a waiter in some pavement café.

Which, by coincidence, is exactly what he did say, a half hour later, to a waiter on the terrace of a very famous café on the Place St Germain where an astonishing number of beautiful, mostly foreign, young girls, ravishing in their light summer dresses and expensive suntans, were watching and being watched by passersby on the hot tree-shaded walk (hard by the news-stand where Bernard bought a copy of *Paris Match* with a stern portrait of General Juin on the cover) – except it was not a Ricard but a *jus d'orange* that he ordered, and a whiskey for Baudoin. The waiter, darkly handsome in a Mediterranean sort of way, substituting for old Hautrive – at that very moment struggling to erect a tent in a high wind on the

Costa Brava – took their order with a distracted air, whistling soundlessly through his teeth and peering over Baudoin's shoulder, pre-occupied as he was by the adorable, bronzed knees of a stunning brunette seated at a table just behind them intently perusing the Secretarial Positions Available column of the *Herald Tribune*.

'*C'est tout simplement incroyable* – I simply don't believe it,' said Baudoin, glancing over his shoulder to see what had fascinated the waiter, 'Gold *Louis* stuffed in the mattress? I thought that was a myth.'

'You'd be surprised,' said Bernard shifting his chair a little bit to the left for a better view of the knees. 'Gold *Louis* is not far off though. The Commander brought back more from his travels than all that bric-à-brac – a nervous party in Saigon entrusted the family fortune to his old friend Commander Vallette just before the Japanese overran it in 1942 – coins mostly and some very valuable trinkets, apparently. He and his family were later killed before they could get away.' Bernard's cigar had gone out. He relit it, extinguishing the match with a symphony conductor's downbeat and dropped it in the ashtray. 'Not in the mattress either. No mattresses for that little old lady. It was in a safe deposit under her maiden name in Carcassonne . . . while it lasted.'

'While it lasted?'

'While it lasted,' repeated Bernard in that irritating way he had. 'The ironic thing is that they were looking for something that no longer existed. We traced the Carcassonne connection by a pure fluke, a bundle of old letters, right under their noses in the bottom drawer of her desk – that wasn't what they were looking for, you see.'

Baudoin visualised a bundle of old letters tied up with a blue ribbon, but couldn't recall where he'd seen them.

'. . . the bank manager was an old flame,' Bernard was saying. 'He probably disposed of it for her as the need arose; she made some bad investments. He's retired now and it was a long time ago – otherwise he might have some embarrassing questions to answer.'

'But why didn't her daughter know it no longer existed?' said Baudoin, exasperated.

'She wasn't supposed to know about it at all! The old lady never told her – who discusses the family finances with an eighteen-year-old? – which is how old she was when she got married and moved to Canada. No – she got the story from the Commander before he died. At that time, it probably was hidden somewhere in the apartment. She was naturally curious about it, although I don't think that was the main reason for her visit, but the widow died before she could bring up the subject. There's no guarantee she would have got an answer anyway. There were strained relations there somewhere. I doubt if the old lady approved of Delpire.' Bernard signalled to the waiter.

'But why couldn't she just inherit legally – why all the elaborate deception?'

'She could have – in principle,' said Bernard. 'Cigar? Non? . . . aside from the fact that there was nothing left to inherit, which they weren't to know, and the fact that the will hasn't been found yet . . . if there is one. They must have searched high and low. It'll probably turn up sooner or later in yet another safe deposit box – very secretive these old birds – long memories . . . Where is that damn waiter? . . . no reason at all, it's perfectly legal in France, to inherit gold. What's more, the taxman will usually turn a blind eye to where it came from if you've held it for more than five years. Establishing that, of course, might have been very difficult and I doubt whether legal niceties much interest Delpire. But all that's academic; that wasn't the problem.' He swivelled round in his chair and rapped on the window behind him.

'Their problem,' put in Baudoin, 'was that they thought . . .'

'. . . *Précisément*,' said Bernard, smiling broadly. 'They thought it was in the apartment, somewhere . . . You see their dilemma.' He smiled broadly.

'They had to find it because . . .'

'. . . because, once her death was recorded, the apartment would become your property. *Voila!* – They could hardly ask your permission to tear it up looking for undeclared gold . . . they had no choice but to conceal her death.' Bernard drew a shiny stripe on the droplet-studded side of the ice bucket and followed appreciatively with his eyes the brunette's departure. 'Forgery, fraud, tax evasion, failure to report a death – and all for something that wasn't there,' he said, lighting up again. 'She may get a suspended sentence, depending on the judge. By the way, Delpire got through most of her bank account. Lucky you live just across the street. I suppose if you hadn't found them out they could have gone on collecting the annuity indefinitely. You might try recovering part of your last quarter's payment, but that might be somewhat embarrassing – you might have to explain to a judge how you got on to them in the first place. Curious. The widow may have been getting a bit gaga. She told her daughter just before she died that she thought she was being followed.'

The waiter finally appeared and Bernard, smiling at Baudoin, ordered another *jus d'orange*.

19

Baudoin removed the faded bouquet of blue iris and, unwrapping a spray of gladioli, placed them in the vase; he stepped back and eyed critically the inscription:

'Commander Eugène Vallette
1885–1944'

Just below was a recently engraved, additional line in slightly brighter gilt. The stone mason had done a good job:

'. . . his beloved wife, Honorine
1887–1957'

He wiped off the marble shelf with his handkerchief, bent down to pick up a piece of string and dust off the toe of his shoe, stepped out and closed the door. There was a slight chill in the air. He turned up the astrakhan collar of the top coat fashioned for him by Lacaussade's tailor in the rue St Florentin and discarding the plastic wrappings, wilted iris and his soiled handkerchief in a refuse bin, descended by the path and along the avenue to the main gate. The taxi was still waiting. Placing a protective hand over his homburg, he slid into the back seat and closed the door. . . . The address which he gave to the driver we do not quite overhear. It may have been Lucette's . . . or, just possibly, Gabrielle's.